MOUTH

JOSHUA HULL

Cover Art by Halil Karasu
Interior Illustrations by Kristofor Harris
Edited by Alex Woodroe

Content warnings are available at the end of this book. Please consult this list for any particular subject matter you may be sensitive to.

TENEBROUS

PRESS

Published by Tenebrous Press.
Visit our website at www.tenebrouspress.com.

First Printing, February 2024.

The characters and events portrayed in this work are fictitious. Any similarity to real persons, living or dead, is coincidental and not intended by the author.

Print ISBN: 978-1-959790-02-0
eBook ISBN: 978-1-959790-03-7

Cover art by Halil Karasu.

Interior illustrations by Kristofor Harris.

Edited by Alex Woodroe.

Formatting by Lori Michelle.

Selected Works from Tenebrous Press:

Lumberjack
a novella by Anthony Engebretson

Posthaste Manor
a novel by Jolie Toomajan & Carson Winter

The Black Lord
a novella by Colin Hinckley

Dehiscent
a novella by Ashley Deng

House of Rot
a novella by Danger Slater

Agony's Lodestone
a novella by Laura Keating

Soft Targets
a novella by Carson Winter

Crom Cruach
a novella by Valkyrie Loughcrewe

Lure
a novella by Tim McGregor

One Hand to Hold, One Hand to Carve
a novella by M.Shaw

More titles at www.TenebrousPress.com

For everyone who has been chewed up by their passion, their love, and their mistakes.

"You have created a monster, and it will destroy you!"
—Doctor Waldman, James Whale's *Frankenstein*

"Everybody has something that chews them up and, for me, that thing was always loneliness. The cinema has the power to make you not feel lonely, even when you are."
—Tom Hanks

RUSTY MEETS MOUTH

RUSTY STOOD NEXT to the grungy old mailbox.

He looked at the name on the side of it. The paint was chipped away but the shadow of the homeowner remained: W. Rogers. He looked at the crumpled diner napkin that had the scribbled address on it. The name *Wayne Rogers* hovered over the destination.

"I guess this is the place," he said out loud to no one in particular.

Rusty didn't have much to his name. He was what you would call *unaffiliated with life*. No commitments. No anything. That was, until he met Wayne Rogers. One strange conversation and a greasy cheeseburger later, Rusty suddenly had a deal in place that would make him a land and homeowner.

That was, if he agreed to take care of Wayne's pet, Mouth.

Easy peasy.

Rusty looked around at the old property. It was in the middle of nowhere and it seemed to go on forever. He hadn't really asked Wayne one single question about it all, so he had no idea what he was walking into.

At least it's a home, he thought. And a home was a nice thing to have again. Even if it looked like some parts of it were crumbling. He stared up at the two-story farmhouse, weeds and more growing all around it. The exterior was covered in multiple colors due to missing paint and weather damage. He planned to fix all of it over time.

Wayne's truck—well, *Rusty's* truck now—was parked in front of the house. That was where Wayne told him his welcome package would be waiting.

Right there in the passenger seat.

Rusty plucked the manilla envelope off the cushion and looked it over. A big, bold **RUSTY** was written on the front in thick, black ink.

"Yep. That's me."

He took a seat on the front steps of the old house, tore open the package and spilled some of the contents into his hand. Multiple keys came tumbling out. He peered inside the tented envelope and a few loose pieces of paper patiently waited. Rusty took the first one out and brought it to his face.

It was a handwritten letter from Wayne.

Hey Rusty,

Welcome to your new life! I hope you didn't think you were getting yourself into a **Pretty Woman** *type scenario. This ain't really that. The house needs work and who knows what all six acres fully look like, but they probably need some love as well.*

This place is yours to do with what you'd like. I can't stop you from taking the deed and selling all of it right now. I could say something like if you did do that, I'd haunt your ass every single day. But I'm not sure how hauntings work or if ghosts are even real.

So, before you go off and do something like that, just do me a favor. Meet Mouth. There's a map in the envelope, it'll take you right to him. Everything else you could possibly need is in there as well. And in the house. Enjoy it all, Rusty. As much as you can. We only get one shot at this adventure. I made plenty of mistakes throughout it all but I'm glad I got to spend the last chapter of my life with Mouth. And I'm glad I asked you to lunch. I'd like to think that I'm making up for some of my wrongs by doing this. Don't let all your wrongs control your life, Rusty.

Take care and enjoy those cheeseburgers!

Sincerely,
Wayne Rogers

Rusty put the letter away and let his face sink. *Was it normal to feel sad about a man you had only met once?*

He hated the feeling of loss. It was why he kept his distance from everyone, he wanted to avoid that feeling completely. He hadn't felt like crying in years, but Rusty wanted to cry like never before as he sat holding onto the last words of a complete stranger who had just signed his entire life over.

He held back the tears and rifled through the other documents in the folder. There was the finalized deed to the land, Rusty's new bank account info, the transferred title to the truck, and a coupon to Sally's Roadside Diner. The last two sheets contained the map to Mouth and a recommended feeding plan.

*Mouth eats once a day. Sometimes you can trap the local exotic wildlife like rabbits and racoons. Easiest meal is just to hop down to Paul's Pets and stock up on some pinky mice. Just tell them you have a large snake. They've never asked me any questions. He eats once a day and I usually try to keep it to around five mice. He does have a very strict diet so keep it simple with mostly mice. He grows too much if it's anything else. So, this means no cats, dogs, or anything like that. He does get a special treat every seven days, but you won't have to worry about that for another five or so days. I left something in the house for you that will explain more. There are a couple of boxes of mice ready to go inside the small barn. Oh, and he enjoys the occasional beer. There's a case in the fridge. **Help yourself.***

Rusty scratched his head at the instructions.

He had been pondering just what kind of animal Mouth was ever since Wayne mentioned him. Up until two seconds ago, he had assumed Mouth was a big dog. Like a Saint Bernard or Rottweiler. Hell, maybe even a wolf. But then Wayne had to go and write *no cats, dogs, or anything like that.* What the hell kind of animal had this man been feeding? A bear? A sasquatch? Rusty had to know, and there was only one way to find out.

He pulled out the map and stared down at the directions that led directly to Mouth.

Rusty shuffled his way through the overgrown property, lugging a box of squeaking mice. He was mostly focused on staying on the makeshift trail Wayne had made.

I should make this a little more accessible, Rusty thought.

But accessible to who?

He wasn't sure.

His dirty old boots were doing a fine job of getting him through the shrubbery. It'd be even easier if he didn't have to lug around the box of critters. He didn't know how much money Wayne left for him, but maybe he could invest in one of those fancy Gators or even a golf cart.

Or maybe he could just stay the course and be grateful that all of *this* belonged to him. Plus, if old man Wayne could make this trek daily, then Rusty didn't have *any* excuse. He didn't mind the outdoors, and it was Fall, so all the trees were starting to change color. It was nice out here. It was—

Rusty found himself standing at the clearing where Mouth lived. There was no animal to be seen. No doghouse, coop, or cave. Only what appeared to be a small sinkhole forming. Confusion took over as he set the box of mice down. He paced around the area, trying to see if he missed anything until—

"Mouth?"

He called out into the wilderness, bracing for anything that could come running toward him. But to his surprise, nothing came. He shouted a few more times, raising his octave with each yell. But still, there was no sign of Mouth anywhere. A horrible feeling swept over Rusty, that he had already let Wayne down on day one. He double checked the map to make sure he was in the right place.

"Where the hell are you?"

He looked down at the box of mice and had an idea. Mouth had spent thirty or so years with Wayne, and Wayne was most likely the only person he ever knew. He was probably shy and scared of an unfamiliar voice. Hell, Rusty would be too. However, Mouth would know the sound of a mouse, and in turn, would hopefully know it was time to eat.

Maybe then he *would* show his face.

Rusty pried open the box and looked down at twenty or so tiny white bodies. Some bounced back and forth, others crawled on the sleeping bodies of their fellow mice. He scooped up one hiding in the cardboard corner and brought it out into the world. Rusty held the little guy with both hands, admiring the small creature.

"Sorry about this, buddy," he said, holding the mouse up into the air with one hand. "Hey Mouth, you hungry???"

As if the little mouse knew what the words meant, it started squeaking with the power of a hundred begging, desperate men. The perfect amount to get the attention of the absent Mouth.

Now, Rusty was waiting for an *animal* to pounce out of the sticks and beg for the small mouse. He wasn't prepared for the ground to shake and erupt with the low hum of a subterranean growl. It rattled him so much, he accidentally lost control of the mouse in his hands. The small creature landed on the ground with a squeaky thud, then rolled over. It shook off the momentary pain and ran toward the hole in the ground.

"Wait!"

Rusty was still trying to wrap his head around the sound and the shaking that came from under his feet. He shook his head and yelled out to the escaping mouse. "Hey! You get back here!" But the mouse ignored Rusty's pleas.

Obviously.

Instead, it continued to run for the sinkhole area that was . . . *slowly closing?*

Rusty took a few steps closer to double check that his eyes weren't playing tricks on him. Sure as hell, the ground was inching shut, giving the mouse more ground to run on. Giving it more room to escape, until both sides retracted back in a vicious snap!

The mouse didn't just fall into the opening; it was engulfed by it. Rusty stopped walking and looked around the area.

What the hell?!

"Did anybody else see that!?"

He looked back at the box of surviving mice.

"Did you guys see that?!"

Of course, there was no answer from Mouth's box lunch.

"Seriously. What the hell was that?!"

Another low rumble from the ground, as if it was answering Rusty's question.

It was meeee.

Rusty collected himself and tapped his jittery fingers against the side of his dirty jeans. Then, he took a few steps forward and nervously peered over the edge of the hole in the ground. His eyes grew wide in shocked horror.

"MOUTH?!"

Rusty stumbled backwards, trying to make sense of what he had just seen. But there was no making sense of something like *that*. The only thing left to do was—

Rusty crumbled to the ground in a passed-out mess.

"No, there was no such thing as an easy way down."

MOUTH

MOUTH STAYED COMPLETELY SILENT.

He was still overwhelmed by what his last friend had done. Mouth hadn't wanted to eat him, but Wayne had just . . . jumped right on in.

Who did that?!

Mouth knew his friend was sick; Wayne told him so every day. So maybe it was supposed to be an easy way out, but there was no such thing as "easy" in there. There was just pain and jagged edges. Wayne probably didn't know that.

Maybe he assumed Mouth was a big passageway into the next world. Like he was just taking a dip into some parallel universe, guarded by a muzzle monstrosity. Or maybe he assumed it was just a normal set of choppers and he could just slide down into the belly of the beast.

Wayne had no way of knowing about all the teeth in the ground.

The ones that curved around his esophagus like a rounded staircase. Each layer serving a different purpose. A function for the madness.

There were the shredders.

The gnawers.

The fangs that could paralyze.

The ones near the bottom that viciously ripped apart whatever chunks of food remained.

Then, there was the actual bottom of Mouth. The place where the soft guts, blood, fur, and goop would pile up. Mouth would discard of the gory mess once every ten days. If you happened to find yourself alive down there, you wouldn't be that way for long.

Mouth's monstrous gastric acid would finish you off.

No, there was no such thing as an easy way down.

Just ask the bevy of mice, rabbits, squirrels, chipmunks, badgers, and whatever else had been unlucky enough to fall inside him. It was one hundred percent a ticket straight to Hell and Wayne had no way of knowing.

Mouth knew that—even though he hadn't wanted to—not only

had he hurt his friend Wayne, but he also had most likely ripped him to shreds. And whatever was left was being pickled in the remnants of gore.

He had hurt the only thing that had ever showed him love and compassion.

And now, he had hurt someone else. Or at least, it certainly felt like he had.

He knew the man fell to the ground because the impact delivered a small tickle at the edge of his maw. And he knew the man must still be sleeping because the only thing he could hear was the swaying of trees and the whining of those small delicious snacks.

Ooooh, he very much wanted more of those!

And he very much wanted another friend. One he hopefully didn't have to eat this time. So Mouth did the only thing he could think to do for attention. He unleashed a massive cry that sounded like a tugboat horn. Then, he shook the ground with the kind of urgency that screamed—

WAKE UP, NEW FRIEND.

MOUTH
IS
IN
THE
GROUND

RUSTY'S EYES SHOT OPEN.

He didn't know if he was screaming before he woke up, or if that started *after*. Same internal debate with his piss-filled jeans. He figured the timeline really didn't matter. He was scared and his crotch was soaked. The cool Fall breeze smacked stone-washed urine against his inner thigh. He hated that feeling. It was cold and uncomfortable and oh yeah—

"Mouth . . . is *in* the ground."

It wasn't exactly a question even though it was a BIG fucking question.

What even is it?

How did it get there?

And why didn't Wayne tell him the truth?

That was one question Rusty had a pretty good answer for.

"Because I would have said *hell no*. That's why!"

The ground rumbled again, startling Rusty. This one was gentler than the one that woke him up a few moments ago. He shot a look at the edge of the opening. Another nervous glance around the woods, then he slowly crawled over to the brim. Another gentle shake vibrated under him. Rusty looked down.

"Mouth? Is that you?"

A friendly rattle of the earth followed, startling Rusty again. He couldn't believe what he was seeing and feeling. Mouth was in the ground. Like, it was some kind of—

The ground rumbled again, snapping Rusty's train of thought. He stared down at the surface and slowly laid flat across it. He touched his cheek to the grass.

"Hello?"

Another playful shake. This one caused a Julia Roberts-esque laugh to escape from Rusty. He was absolutely horrified but found himself completely fascinated by the thing.

He pulled himself off the ground and peered over the edge. He knew *this* would be one of those moments in a monster movie where the camera pulled back to show the full scope of Rusty standing over the five foot opening.

And Mouth did look like he was straight out of a monster movie.

The interior of the hole looked like the inside of a leatherback sea turtle's mouth. Sharp teeth were on all sides. It was terrifying to stand over, so he took a safe step back from the edge. The ground rumbled again, as if it was telling Rusty he was safe.

"You don't want to eat me?"

Another rumble from the terrain.

Nooooo.

Rusty put his hands on his hips and let out a deep sigh of relief. "That's, um, good to hear." He stared down into Mouth until the squeaking of the mouse box pulled his focus.

Right.

"You're probably hungry. Want to, ummm, eat?"

The surface shook with excitement. Rusty let out a small, uncomfortable laugh, as if he had to calm down an excited, hungry dog jumping up on him. He walked over and picked up the Pete's Pets container, then returned to the edge of the gap. He looked down into the box as the gang of mice scurried around.

"This is so weird. Sorry, little guys."

Then, with a slight hesitation, he poured a dozen mice into the hole.

Mouth gnashed and gobbled the critters in a bloody, bony flurry. Rusty watched as Mouth swallowed the mice like a garbage disposal eliminating food waste. A few moments later, Mouth let out what could only be described as a ground burp. It was followed by a thankful rumble of the earth. Rusty shook his head in disbelief.

"You're welcome. I'm Rusty by the way."

The earth shuddered back.

I'm Mouth.

Rusty nodded and brought the empty mouse box down to his side. He looked the wet mess of himself over, then peered deep into the teeth-filled hole.

"You made me piss myself, Mouth."

The ground shook with subterranean laughter. Rusty couldn't help but join in.

The next few weeks went about the same for Rusty and Mouth. Fewer nerves and half the piss. It was hard to wrap his head around the fact that he already had dumped three crates of mice into the beast. That was around a hundred or so of the little critters used as a fast-food snack pack.

Rusty let out a small laugh thinking about this weird new direction his life had taken.

Last month, he was hitchhiking up and down the local highway, rinsing scrambled egg-covered plates, trying to forget all the things that had led him there. Now, he was the only caretaker for this monster in the woods. His face scrunched up.

Rusty felt bad about calling Mouth a monster.

He didn't know anything about the underground behemoth, so it felt wrong to refer to it in a harmful way. Mouth was a living being, just like him. Sure, they looked different and ate different. But they were both alive and they were both unique.

What's so monstrous about that?

Although Rusty really didn't consider the term monster to be a negative. Growing up, it was always a badge of honor. Rusty's mom introduced him to old horror movies at a young age. He vividly remembered those nights where they'd watch old black and white films.

Those marathons included Hammer Horror titles like *Horror of Dracula* or *The Curse of Frankenstein*. The two of them cheered over a bootleg VHS copy of Tod Browning's *Freaks*. Rusty hid behind a pillow during the original Steve McQueen-led *The Blob*. And they loved watching the classic Universal Monster movies. Rusty's mom had grown up watching them on Sammy Terry's *Nightmare Theater*, so she wanted him to do the same.

He loved them all. He gravitated more toward James Whale's *Frankenstein*, but he *always* connected with them all. Those characters were almost always mistreated and misunderstood. Perceived as an ugly stain on humanity. Despite that, Rusty always saw the beauty in the beasts and even though the teeth in the ground looked like they could eat the world, he saw that same beauty in Mouth. He now had his very own universal monster.

And it was his job to keep the angry village as far away as possible.

THE MEDDLING ABIGAIL GATES

ABIGAIL **GATES USED** to trust people.

Heck, she used to *like* people, but then they'd always let her down. It was exhausting to always feel like the next scammer or abuser was right around the corner. That was part of the reason why she had left home when she was sixteen.

Her happy Indiana life was one big lie.

Her dad had died when she was just two years old, so of course her mom would remarry by the time she entered elementary school. And of course, she had to marry the principal of said elementary school. She was pretty sure Bob the Principal always wanted to be a drill sergeant but somehow ended up policing snot nosed kids every single day. He hated it, so he took it out on the one snot nosed kid he could. And Abigail's mom let him. Not like *she* had much of a choice either.

That cycle continued with classmates, girlfriends, and boyfriends. By the time high school came around, she had earned the nickname of "Abiwail" because of her constant crying. Her only safe place was her relatively plain bedroom that had a box filled with cinematic magic.

She had found the big box of VHS tapes hidden away in the basement. Bob was intent on purging their house of every relic Abigail's father had left behind; but luckily, she got to the tapes and the old VCR before he did. And that was where she'd discover the magic of movies.

The original *Star Wars* trilogy, *The Goonies*, the *Indiana Jones* trilogy, *Gremlins*, *Labyrinth*, *Ghostbusters*, *Stand by Me*, *Close Encounters of the Third Kind*, and more. Eventually, her attention and eyes started to gravitate to horror titles and their cover art.

Movies like *The Evil Dead*, *Halloween*, *Bad Taste*, *Poltergeist*, Cronenberg's *The Fly*, and other horrific offerings. She even liked *Halloween III: Season of the Witch* before it was considered cool to do so. She watched *everything*, and before long, she decided that would be her path in life. She wanted to make movies. Not just for her, but for her dad.

That would show Bob the Prick Principal!

Until, well, he had showed *her*, by trashing the entire collection. So the only way to respond was to run away and head for Los Angeles like a character from *The Wizard*.

She made it all the way to Dillsboro, Indiana. A little less than two hours away from where she started.

She had zero savings, so she lived in her car. She bounced around from job to job, hoping to stay employed past the first week. There was the laundromat, the grocery store, and the gas station with the peculiar attendant with one arm. She was fired from all three jobs in a four-week span. Luckily, she had managed to secure a cheap duplex and a lead on a new job.

Part-time clerk at Paul's Pets. Which had recently shifted to full-time clerk still at part-time pay. She didn't mind the hours. The store was slow, and she was mostly the only one there. It gave her plenty of time to play with the animals and brainstorm schlocky horror movie ideas. It also gave her plenty of time to pay attention to the local weirdos doing weird things.

And she was absolutely certain that Rusty was a weirdo person doing weirdo shit. Why else would he be going through boxes of mice on a weekly basis?

"Dude, you know there are other snake owners in this town, right?"

She watched as Rusty looked her over, caught off guard by the accusatory statement from the Paul's Pets clerk. She noticed his face slightly light up at the sight of some of her horror themed tattoos.

"Oh, well. Umm. It's big and it likes to eat."

"Like Jennifer Lopez, Ice Cube kind of big? Because . . . that's what *this* feels like," she leaned down on the counter, closer to the suspicious Rusty. "It also sort of feels like you might be making those stomping videos. Do you own a pair of high heels?"

He shook his head, awkwardly doing his best to hide any strange or suspicious reaction. She watched as he nervously tried to find something to change the topic to. He landed on the tattoo of an older scientist-looking man holding a brain next to a shirtless corpse.

"I, umm, like your *Frankenstein* tattoo."

Abigail grinned, slightly impressed by the fact the weirdo man knew exactly what the ink was supposed to be.

"You know who that is?"

Rusty delivered a quick nod. "That was my favorite movie growing up. Why'd you go with Dr. Frankenstein instead of—"

"Instead of Frankenstein's Monster? Well, because people are just going to say they like my *Frankenstein* tattoo regardless. So, I wanted them to actually be right for once."

She shrugged as she rang up the mice.

"Have they been?"

Abigail let out a slightly embarrassed laugh that turned into disappointment.

"Nope. You're the first person to get it."

Rusty sighed, sharing in her disappointment. "Men. How ignorant art thou."

He smiled and took out his wallet, handing her his bank card. She gave a nod, swiped the plastic, and handed it back. Then, she pushed the last box of mice his way.

"See you in a few days, Anaconda."

She watched as Rusty gave a nervous nod and walked out of the shop. She had now sold him five boxes of mice every week for the last month. The math didn't add up in her head. Even if Rusty had a *large* ball python, it would only need to eat once a week. And one to two mice at that. No, something wasn't right here.

Abigail Cates used to be curious, and that curiosity was back in a BIG way. She wasn't going to see Rusty in a few days. She was going to see him in a few minutes . . . from a safe distance.

She followed the old pickup truck as far as she could.

Rusty had turned into his driveway, and Abigail couldn't exactly follow him by car. So she had to park and walk the rest of the way. Luckily for her, the property was surrounded by woods. She could keep a safe distance while using the trees for cover.

She watched as Rusty put four of the mice boxes in the barn next to the house. He returned to the truck to grab the fifth one. Before walking off, Rusty looked around, as if he could feel someone watching him. Abigail dipped behind a tree, hiding as best she could.

Moments later, she was carefully tracking him from inside the brush. She wasn't worried about always keeping her eyes on him because she didn't have to. She could just follow the sounds of the squeaking mice.

Where the hell was he taking them?

She creeped closer to the loud squeaks of the mouse box. It sounded like they were suddenly scared. A few more steps and she could see Rusty standing in a clearing. He was talking to someone *. . . or something?* Her curiosity got the better of her and she pulled herself out into the clearing, just as Rusty dumped some of the mice into a hole.

"So . . . this is where you keep Mega Snake, huh?"

He stared back at her in full-blown shock. "Did you follow me here?!"

"Umm, obviously. Yes."

"That's . . . pretty messed up!" He moved the box behind his back. She rolled her eyes and pointed at it.

"Are you trying to hide that box from me?"

Rusty looked around, then shook his head. "What box?"

"That one, man!" She kept her eyes locked on him as he slowly pulled the box back out. Abigail folded her arms, then shook her head.

"What kind of weirdo shit are you doing out here with our mice? You trying to build a rat king or something?"

Rusty shook his head at the ridiculous accusation. He shook his head at everything. He was going to have to lie again, even though he was absolute shit at it.

"That's . . . where the snake lives."

Abigail sized him up as she got closer.

"I need to see it for myself . . . or I'm blocking all further mice purchases."

Rusty's eyes went small with doubt. "Can you even do that?"

"I'm practically the manager. I can do whatever I want. So . . . ?"

Rusty took a deep swallow, then paced around nervously. Abigail watched as he had a small conversation with himself. She used it to her advantage, moving closer to the hole in the ground. He turned to finally reply, then realized she was already at the edge, staring down into Mouth. "Don't loo—"

"What the fuck is that thing?!"

But before Rusty could answer, the ground rumbled beneath her feet and knocked the meddling Abigail Cates off balance.

MOUTH WAS ANNOYED

MOUTH WAS ANNOYED.

He didn't get to enjoy the small creatures he liked so much because of the new voice yelling at his friend Rusty. He missed the first bite, which was one of his favorite parts of feeding time. Sure, he could taste them all the way down, but it was that *very* first taste that Mouth loved.

It made him feel alive. Mouth liked that feeling. He didn't know why, but there was something about fear that made things taste better. At least that's what Wayne used to say.

He wondered what this new voice tasted like.

Mouth didn't like the way Rusty sounded. Like he was scared or nervous. And he *definitely* didn't like the way the new voice was talking to his friend. Luckily, he could feel the voice getting closer to his teeth. *Why wasn't Rusty stopping it?*

Oh! Maybe . . . maybe his new friend Rusty wanted him to eat this new voice!

His old friend Wayne would occasionally bring him voices. Maybe that's what *this* was. Another special treat! Mouth loved the way the voices tasted . . . except for Wayne, of course. He tasted different from the others. Not as fresh.

But Mouth was excited to see what this one tasted like! He rumbled with excitement as the new voice peered over the edge.

"What the fuck is that thing?!"

It's me. The teeth in the ground.

ABIGAIL
MEETS
MOUTH

RUSTY STARED BACK.

He didn't know why the young girl with the Dr. Frankenstein tattoo followed him home. He didn't know why she followed him all the way out to the clearing in the woods. What he did know was that she couldn't see Mouth. That would be . . . *problematic*. He went back and forth with himself, trying to make a decision that made the most sense.

Should he give her money?

Should he tell her the truth?

Should he feed her to Mouth?

He covered his mouth in horror at that last thought. Sure, the girl was rude for following him home, and she was abrasive as heck. But that didn't mean she should be prepped and served up to the abnormal trap in the ground. He should just talk to her.

Yeah, that's what I'll do.

I'll just try and reason with—

He turned to see Abigail was already standing at the edge of Mouth. *Oh shit.*

"Don't loo—"

Abigail looked back at him in absolute horror. "What the fuck is that thing?!"

Rusty tried to form the right answer in his head. *Well, it's a subterranean mouth monster that I was bequeathed by a strange old man. I feed him once a day and I think he's my best friend.*

He shook his head. That was *not* the way to go. He racked his head for a different answer.

That thing is none of your fucking business. Now retreat, you nosey juvenile!

Another shake of the head. There had to be a better way to tell her—

Suddenly, the ground rumbled with excitement, knocking Abigail off balance. She screamed out, on the verge of tumbling into the massive chomping hole that was Mouth. Rusty watched as the new awkward situation he had found himself in was being handled by the teeth in the ground.

No need to tell her anything if she was just going to be ground food. *Problem solved!*

He watched as she wavered, the earth continuing to rattle her closer to the edge. He slowly raised both hands up to cover his guilty eyes. He couldn't bear to watch this poor girl be devoured by Mouth. He also didn't want to *hear* her be devoured but the good lord had only gifted him with two hands.

Another hard choice and another external debate with himself.

"Help!" Abigail screamed out.

Rusty looked over at her in shock.

Right. That, of course, was a third option. He didn't have to worry about covering his eyes or ears if he just helped the poor girl. That would open a whole new can of worms, but it was better than watching, or hearing, the girl be scarfed down.

At least, he hoped it was.

He rushed over and grabbed onto her just as she was about to tumble over the edge. The ground continued to rumble beneath their feet, bringing both of them closer to the brim of the hole. Closer to a painful descent into a pearly white hell. Finally, Rusty screamed out—

"No, Mouth!"

Then, the ground went as still and silent as can be. The sudden stop knocked both Rusty and Abigail to the ground. Mouth had listened. *He listened!* Rusty let out a small laugh and exhaled in relief.

"Thank you, Mouth!"

Rusty turned to see Abigail glaring at him. He noticed her scowl and took a nervous gulp.

"Are you okay?" He sheepishly asked.

"No, dude. I'm *not* okay! Seriously. What. The. Fuck. Is. That. Thing?!"

Another nervous swallow from Rusty—

"That's Mouth."

The odd pair stared out over the teeth in the ground.

After Abigail finally calmed down and agreed not to call the police or the news or anyone else, Rusty told her how he had come to take care of Mouth.

"If it makes you feel better, I thought it was just going to be a big dog." Rusty said, attempting to make peace as he nervously drummed the outside of his jeans. She looked at him, confused by the statement.

"What kind of dog has a daily diet of mice?"

Rusty scratched his head. "A big, mean one?"

She shook her head and peered over the edge into Mouth. The teeth stared back, silent as can be. "Old Man Rogers left you in charge of your very own Sarlaac Pit. That's wild."

She looked up to see Rusty staring back at her, a slightly bewildered face. "Oh sorry. The Sarlaac Pit is this thing in—"

He cut her off. "*Return of the Jedi*, I know. I'm just . . . How old are you again?"

Abigail scoffed at his question.

"That's not a great question for a drifting stranger like yourself to ask young women, buddy."

Rusty gave a nod, and a silent apology. "You're right. Sorr—"

"I'm nineteen."

"And you know what *Return of the Jedi* is?"

She started walking around the outline of Mouth, fascinated by the creature, less fascinated by Rusty. He was different than any of the men she knew or had known. There was a kindness to him. More importantly, there wasn't a single hint of creep to be found. Just obliviousness.

"I'm sorry, you're surprised that I know about a *Star Wars* movie? It's *Star Wars*, dude. I'm going to really blow your mind when I talk about this crazy old movie called *Jaws*." She delivered a shit-eating grin at Rusty. He was still scratching his head. "I'm fucking with you, man. Movies are sort of my thing."

"Your thing?"

"Yeah. My passion. My dream. My biggest love." She continued to patrol every side of mouth.

"Oh, okay. That's . . . neat."

She stared back at Rusty from across the gap in his land.

"It *is* neat. Hey, want to know a fun fact about this town that you now call home?" She said, a sly grin spread across her face.

"Sure, I guess," Rusty said, scratching his head.

Abigail's eyes lit up like she was about to deliver a scary story around a campfire. She even dipped her voice into a lower octave to fit the part.

"This town has an urban legend that some old B-movie filmmaker from the seventies quit Hollywood and moved here. Except, he didn't stop making films. He'd kidnap loners, people just passing through. Transients like you, Rust. And those poor bastards would find themselves the shining stars of his snuff films. Crazy, right?"

"That's not true."

"It is! One of them escaped and told the entire tale! Said the guy had a pet he fed people to on camera. Most assumed it was a big, mean dog like Cujo or something. But what if it wasn't a dog?"

Abigail stared down into Mouth with big, curious eyes.

"I don't believe you or that crazy story."

"I'm just saying, Rust. Urban legends start somewhere. I bet it was Mouth."

She grinned like she was about to add on to her theory . . . but someone else did first. The ground shook; not with excitement, but with caution. There hadn't been a rumble like that before.

They both looked down at the teeth in the ground.

"What was that?" Abigail nervously asked.

"Oh, I should have explained that. It's how he talks to me. Talks to . . . *us?*"

Her eyes grew wide. "Do you know anything about *that* story, Mouth?"

The area fell into complete silence until another cautious rumble shook the ground.

Yes.

Rusty and Abigail looked at each other, their faces both growing in separate reactions. His in horror, and hers in excitement.

"Holy shit, dude. Do you know what this means?" Abigail said, joy spilling out behind her words. **The ground shook again—**

Mouth knew *exactly* what it meant.

GOONIE
SHIT

RUSTY TRIED HIS best to keep up with the boisterous nineteen-year-old.

His damn near fifty-year-old knees couldn't move with the same speed and force. He watched as Abigail ran practically at a full sprint to his house from deep in the woods. He could barely keep up with his half-assed jog. *Was it even a jog at that point?* It felt like he was limping more than usual. His chest hurt and he was fighting for his breath. He'd be no good to Mouth dead.

Hell, all of this was no good.

Rusty slowed to his normal walk. He knew where his house was, and Abigail would have to wait for him, anyway; he had locked the door before heading off to the pet store earlier. He was suddenly reminded of the fact that the pet store clerk he was chasing to his house had followed him home. Was he just supposed to forget that little fact ever happened? Because of some tall tale? *Screw that!*

Rusty was grumpy and in pain. Every little ache in his knees made him regret saving Abigail from falling into Mouth. She was completely out of sight now. Probably casing the outside of his house.

My house, he thought. Yep. Still weird.

Every once in a while he heard Abigail call out something like, *Hurry up,* or *Where are you?* He tried to ignore her, but that could only last for so long.

Rusty came out of the woods to see Abigail sitting on the porch steps. Frustration was written all over her face.

"Dude, could you hurry it up. I think I turned twenty-one just waiting for you."

He stared back and folded his arms, trying to catch his breath.

"Not until you tell me why you came out here."

A gigantic sigh escaped her mouth, and she jumped up. "Isn't it obvious, man? I thought you were full of shit. And that should be okay . . . because you were! Snakes don't eat that much. But bygones, dude! Because now you and I are on a quest."

Rusty's hands fell back to the side of his body. They tapped his legs for a moment, then once again folded across his chest. "We're on a what?"

"A quest. An adventure. You know, like *The Goonies*. But if *The Goonies* was about murder."

He shook his head. "*The Goonies was* about murder, Abigail."

Abigail's head dropped in shame. "No, dude. *The Goonies* was about—"

"Oh, right. *Treasure.*"

"Yes, but no. The treasure was each other and their families. That's why the real shit didn't matter in the end, even though it saved *everything*. But that doesn't matter! *The Goonies* were determined to find out the truth about their town and by doing so, found out the truth about themselves. Ta-da! That's us *right* now. But also, yes, there was a murder in the goondocks."

Rusty scratched his head and tried to form a string of proper words. After an awkward cycle of weird poses, he finally landed back on his folded arms and confused face.

"Are you saying we're *The Goonies* in this situation."

Abigail smiled as wide as can be. "We already have a Mouth."

Abigail rifled through Rusty's pantry, her stomach burning with hunger.

"How long have you lived here again?" she asked, pulling a saltine cracker out of its plastic sleeve and popping it in her mouth.

"Maybe a month."

She spun around, delivering a *you-have-to-be-joking* glare. "You need to go shopping or get some food delivered. These crackers are stale as shit." She popped another stale-as-shit cracker into her mouth.

"They were already here."

She gagged and let a mouthful of cracker bits spill out. "Gross." Then, after a moment of contemplation, she shoved another stale cracker in her mouth.

"Stop eating them," Rusty said with a baffled look on his face.

"I'm hungry. I missed my lunch break following you all the way out here."

She set the sleeve of stale crackers down on the kitchen counter.

"Well, whose fault is that?" Rusty said.

"Yours, obviously. You *were* full of shit."

Rusty shook his head and let out a sigh. "I was just doing what Wayne told me to do."

"Wayne. You know that's probably a bullshit name, right?"

She continued to investigate the kitchen, occasionally opening cabinets and slamming them shut. Rusty stood his ground.

"It's on all the paperwork."

She spun around, rolling her eyes. "That's because he couldn't put his real name on everything. Not a lot of bank accounts active under the name *Dillsboro Death Dealer*."

He shook his head. "What is that?"

"That's what they call him around here, man! Keep up." She entered the living room. "Want to hear my theory?"

Rusty sighed. "No, I do not."

"Cool cool cool," Abigail nodded. "So basically, I think he would bring them out there and do weirdo shit to them . . . then feed them to Mouth when he was all done."

"Weirdo shit?"

She raised her eyebrows in a flurry of up and downs. "Yeah, you know, weirdo shit."

"I really didn't want to hear that, Abigail."

"Because you know it's fucking true, Rusty Rust."

Rusty let out a deep sigh.

He was used to silence in his life. He only had to deal with Wayne for one lunch hour and a boring bank meeting. Sure, it was a little strange, but it was nowhere near the hell this was. Abigail was like if the energizer bunny hosted a murder podcast and never hit stop on the *Record* button.

She was overwhelming and brought chaotic energy into his life. Hell, not even the damn teeth in the ground did that. And now she had this crackpot theory about Wayne's secret life. Rusty had to get her out of this house.

"Listen, I really need—"

Abigail spun around and folded her arms. She was waiting for some bullshit excuse from the same guy who lied about feeding mice to a pet snake. He could tell that her BS meter was already flickering off the charts.

"To run to the bathroom." He let out a sigh and turned for the hallway.

"Hey Rusty—"

He stopped and turned back to the exhausting young woman in his house. "Yeah?"

"Where's that door go to?" She pointed to an area right outside of the living room. He joined her and stared.

"Maybe the basement? I don't really know."

Abigail let loose the sound of frustration. "You don't know?!"

"Listen, kid—"

"Don't do that." She said, glaring at him like never before.

This one was even worse than the one she gave when Mouth nearly ate her. He adjusted his stance and sized Abigail up. Rusty wasn't good at talking to people, but he was good at knowing when he had crossed a line. He did a lot of that in his old life. He didn't mean anything negative by calling her a "kid". It was just a saying, something older folks like him said to younger folks like her.

"I didn't mean anything by it. I was just going to say—"

"What were you going to say, Adult?" Her irritation was still as clear as day. Rusty sighed and took the jab.

"If you couldn't tell by my roaming lifestyle, I'm not exactly good at talking to people. Plus, it's not like I've been checking out every nook and cranny in this place."

"Why the hell not? It's your house. Have you never been to a hotel or anything? That's the first thing you do. Open all the doors and find all the shit."

Rusty shifted his stance, feeling the sting of the comment.

"I'm used to . . . simpler things. *All this?* A house, responsibility, a Mouth to feed. It's all so new to me. Look, I haven't had any doors to open in a very long time, Abigail."

He watched as she tilted her head, then gave a "that's that!" nod.

"Well then, it's time for some Goonie shit, Rusty. Want to open some doors together?"

IN

THE

MOUTH

OF

MYSTERY

ABIGAIL **WAS THE** first one to reach the basement floor.

She felt around the old musty room until she found the pull string light in the middle of the space. She pulled the string and crossed her fingers, hoping that the cobweb-covered bastard would work.

After a few flickers of half-life, the old light bulb came to life and lit the dingy joint up. She turned and smiled at Rusty, who now stood at the bottom of the steps.

"It's alive!!" She laughed at herself, then started investigating the space.

It was filled with old furniture and boxes, each one labeled with different holidays or contents. She opened a box with Christmas written on the side and peered into it. There was nothing inside. She pushed the box away and kept looking.

Rusty investigated the other side of the basement. Stacked chairs sat next to a piano covering a big chunk of the wall. Boxes and other clutter crowded every space of the instrument. Abigail noticed it and walked over to get a better look.

"Holy shit, dude. *Mozart lived here!*"

She watched as Rusty shook his head at her sarcasm and went back to focusing on the boxes. "There's nothing in them."

Abigail perked up at Rusty's news.

"Umm. The Christmas box was empty."

They both looked at each other, then knocked the empty boxes off the top of the piano. A massive smile filled Abigail's face as the outline of a smaller door was suddenly visible.

"Well, well, well. Would you look at that?"

Rusty looked down to see clear scrape marks on the floor from the bottom of the piano. The stains of a secret room. He grabbed the corner of the piano and pulled it out, matching it up with the previous marks on the ground. He took a step back and stood next to Abigail, who was grinning at the sight of the newly revealed door. They looked at each other and smiled.

"Goonie shit."

Rusty sighed. "You're enjoying this way too much."

"Yes, I am. This has turned into a legit quest, my guy."

Rusty wasn't sure how he felt now. All of this was new to him, and he liked his lifetime habit of leaving well enough alone. He wanted to just move the piano back and get Abigail the hell out of there. He didn't even know if he cared what was behind that door. This was *his* house now; he could just leave that door closed forever and never have a second thought about it.

Unless, of course, the rumors were true.

And Wayne, *or whatever the hell his name was*, had some poor vagrant chained up in there. That would be hard to live with. But then again, it would be a huge problem for both him and Abigail. They'd have to explain to the police why they were down there in the first place. And *if* there was a vagrant chained up, they would most certainly find out about the existence of Mouth.

It was a real predicament for a man newly in charge of a subterranean cakehole.

"Wait, what if someone's in there?" He asked, just as she was about to open the door.

"Then we should probably get them out?"

"Wouldn't that cause us even more issues?" Rusty said, scratching the side of his neck. Abigail stared back at the baffled adult in front of her. She took her hand off the doorknob and placed it on his shoulder.

"Look, man. Let's deal with one thing at a time. Best case, the room is empty. Worst case? It's stockpiled with the victims of the *Dillsboro Death Dealer*, and you were just gifted a real house of fucking horror. Who knows what's actually in there? This guy seems to be a bit of a weirdo, right? Remember, he *did* bestow you an actual horrific mouth in the ground. So, he definitely liked his secrets."

She was one hundred percent right. It couldn't get much weirder than a mouth in the ground. Rusty let out a sigh of relief and nodded. She took her hand off his shoulder and let out a small laugh.

"Alright, contestant Rust. You ready to see what's behind door number one?"

He delivered his nervous seal of approval, so Abigail gave the knob a slight turn. Much to their surprise, the door opened with relative ease. They both took a deep breath and entered the dark room.

"You see anything?" she asked.

"No, nothing."

Another small laugh from Abigail. "Well, bonus points. We don't hear anyone begging for their life."

The pair spent another few moments feeling around in the dark until—

"I think I found the light switch," said Rusty. In a moment the small hidden room was illuminated. It took a moment for their eyes to adjust to the new lighting, but once they had, it was full *holy-shit-what-have-we-uncovered* mode. Rusty looked over at the grinning face of Abigail.

"What did I tell you, dude? The motherfucking Dillsboro Death Dealer."

THE MOTHER FUCKING DILLSBORO DEATH DEALER

WILLIAM **REED MADE** his first movie with his father's 8mm camera when he was eight years old.

It starred his toy dinosaurs and his collection of plastic army men. The prehistoric beasts stomped across the ground—with the help of a human hand wrapped around their torsos—trouncing on and kicking the little green guys out of the way. William even managed to have the giant lizards chomp down on a few unlucky soldiers, thanks to the magic of stop motion and, once again, his human hand.

From there, he graduated to cheesy horror makeup and paying his friends in soda and pizza to be able to kill them on camera. Once he was in high school, he focused his attention, and lens, on the many attractive students walking the halls of the campus. William Reed wasn't easy on the eyes, but his camera was. And his classmates liked the way it made them look.

Even if they didn't particularly like *him*.

After graduation in 1965, he left his small town and headed out west for Hollywood. William wanted to be the next John Ford, but he'd gladly accept being next in line for Roger Corman over at New World Pictures. He knew the famous B-movie producer loved giving young new names a chance with film projects, and William planned on being one of them.

Unfortunately, he never even got close to Corman or New World Pictures.

He instead found production work on even lower budget films for a company making movies outside of Los Angeles called Cyclops Pictures. The not-so-inside joke was that their movies would be *much* better if you watched them with just one eye. Cyclops had titles like *Attack of the Bare Foot Babes*, *Brontosaurus Babylon*, *Killer Couch Potato*, and *Biker Swordsmen of the S.S.*

William Reed was far from *The Grapes of Wrath* or *Stagecoach* territory. But he was in California working on motion pictures. That *was* his dream.

William finally gained the trust of Mr. Cyclops Pictures

himself, Rand Myers, in the late sixties with a Western pitch called *A Dude Named Utah*. The project was pitched as a love letter to the likes of John Ford and John Wayne, and followed a drifter named Utah out for revenge against the settlers who had killed his family while he was out looking for gold.

It was to be a good old-fashioned Western picture.

Reed was convinced he could get an indie actor named Dennis Hopper to star as the dude named Utah, since Hopper was just making LSD-filled movies across town for Corman. He planned on making *Utah* a star vehicle for the young Hopper.

The green, twentysomething William Reed had pie in the sky aspirations for the Western project. He was so blinded by his vision, he had no idea Hopper was set to co-write, star, and direct a little movie called *Easy Rider*. That hippy fucker wasn't about to follow it up with a love letter to the old guard of Hollywood. *He hated the old guard!*

Without Hopper, *Utah* was put into temporary turnaround.

Rand Myers followed the decision up with a unique offer for Reed. If he wanted to eventually direct *A Dude Named Utah*, he had to direct two other movies for Cyclops Pictures. The first was a sequel to their 1959 dinosaur utopia bomb *Brontosaurus Babylon*, aptly titled *Brontosaurus Babylonia*. The second film would be decided on at a later date, but it had to be whatever Rand and Cyclops wanted.

There would be zero negotiations.

If Rand wanted William Reed to direct a caveman porno movie, then Reed was going to have to direct the hell out of it. If they wanted him to take a camera crew and camp out at the Mount of Olives waiting for the resurrection of Christ, just so they could crucify him on camera this time, then by God, *and literally by God*, they would be there waiting for fucking magic hour.

There wouldn't be the possibility to direct something like *The Searchers* for William Reed unless he made whatever Cyclops schlock was demanded of him. So Reed accepted the terms of the deal, because even if the second movie was an abysmal concept, he'd still be making movies. And again, that was the dream, right?

To make movies.

To be a working filmmaker.

Plus, he basically had already made *Brontosaurus Babylonia* on his father's 8mm camera when he was a young boy. In William's eyes, the guarantee of being an actual working filmmaker was better than having artistic integrity.

If only Rand's contract and Cyclops Pictures had integrity.

Rand tinkered with the wording of the contract to trap William Reed into making at least *four* movies of their choice before they would even consider financing *A Dude Named Utah*. How? By adding in a contractual component that the movies had to be deemed a success to count. And when you're Rand Myers and Cyclops Pictures, and you're in charge of your own product, you get to decide what's a success.

And what's a massive failure.

So, William Reed went from pie-in-the-sky, *two-for-them, one-for-me* aspirations, to being trapped in a contract with the scum of all scum. Once he realized this, he started doing three things.

First, he started saving his money.

Second, he began looking for property far away from Hollywood. Even though he hadn't *actually* experienced making movies in Hollywood. He was done with the whole damn dream. He didn't even want to *think* about John Ford anymore, let alone *be* him.

The third thing he started doing was drinking. A lot. He was blackout drunk for the entire third movie he "made" for Cyclops Pictures. A *Blob* rip-off called *Hair Ball*, about a rampaging hairball that would engulf people. Reed was sure the entire movie was a massive "fuck you" and a big write-off. It was solely made for the purpose of laughing at William.

Next came a clear rip-off of Michel Levesque's *Werewolves on Wheels* called *Cycle Ghouls*. That was a cheesy biker movie about a gang of ghosts in cheap Ben Cooper-like ghost masks. And just like ghosts, William wished people couldn't see the movie. But at the end of the day, he also didn't give a shit.

He was blind drunk and planning his escape, fulfilled contract or not.

William Reed liked to visit Indiana because it reminded him of Morton DaCosta's 1962 film, *The Music Man*. Specifically Gary,

Indiana. He wasn't a big fan of musicals, but his mother was, so Indiana always made him think of her. He'd find himself smiling whenever the song "Gary, Indiana" popped into his head.

It was during one of these memory-fueled trips through the heartland when William Reed drove through the town of Dillsboro. It was a small town with what appeared to be a very small population. And it had an old farmhouse sitting on seven acres for sale.

Dillsboro was about as far away from Hollywood as you could get, so William Reed used a chunk of his filmmaking savings and bought the house and land. It was relatively cheap compared to the small dump he called home in California. Cheaper even than a Rand Myers picture! He was so desperate to make his escape from Cyclops Pictures that he barely gave the place a look-over. There was a house and there was land. That's all William Reed needed to start over.

And start over he did.

He began with monthly trips, filling his luggage with whatever he could to make the big move as hassle-free as possible. He would work on the house, giving it new paint and a good cleanup. He'd walk the grounds, slowly clearing a path through his seven acres. Hell, he even sobered up for the most part. He'd still drink out in California because that was the only way for him to get through production on *The Green Stink*.

It was supposed to be Cyclops offering some sort of commentary on how poisoned the climate was getting, but instead, it just ended up being about a green, toxic cloud that didn't even operate half the time. And unlike that Steven kid who benefited from a similar situation at Martha's Vineyard, Rand and Cyclops forced William to keep the green cloud in every single shot it was supposed to be in. Nothing says horror like your stars screaming in terror at a mechanical cloud barely chugging along. The fucker wasn't even green. It was a mix of brown and gray that didn't even light up properly. William was thankful when that piece of shit wrapped.

It was going to be his last movie for Rand Myers and Cyclops Pictures. Or at least that's what he thought. It wasn't until the courier dropped off a batch of new screenplays, each emblazoned with the familiar Cyclops logo. Reed flipped through the bundle like a confused school child. The stack contained five titles: *Hair Ball 2*, *Hair Ball 3: Scary Harry*, *The Green Stink Strikes Again*, and something called *Bambi and the Blood Thirsty Bimbos*. The cover page had an illustrated brassiere with two fang bites on the left side.

He opened the screenplay to see a handwritten note from Myers himself. *Get to work. You owe us five more pictures to fulfill your contract. Oh . . . and they'll be pro bono because of how bad the others did. Sincerely, A Dude Named Rand.*

William's blood burned at the note, especially with the way he signed his name. He was never going to be free of Rand and Cyclops. There was only one way out of this entire mess, even if it was earlier than planned. Reed knew that now. He spent all night loading up a trailer and left town like he was a member of the Baltimore Colts. Nobody was going to know where William Reed was headed because William Reed would soon be no more.

Back home in Indiana, William continued to work on clearing out the overgrown acreage. It was during one of these clearing sessions that a wild rabbit startled him as it ran from the brush. Reed grabbed his chest and laughed as the small rodent took off running.

Here he was, a genre filmmaker scared by a little ole rabbit! He settled down and went back to his clearing when suddenly, the painful screams of that same rabbit rang out. Reed took a few steps and saw what was happening.

The bottom half of the rabbit was stuck in a tiny hole. Except, it didn't appear to just be stuck. Something was *eating* it; or at least that's what all the blood made it seem like. William took a few more steps and saw that the rabbit was buried up to its torso.

It was *definitely* being eaten alive.

Reed couldn't take the sounds anymore, so he grabbed a rake and whacked the animal on the head. No more screams, but whatever was eating the poor thing just kept on chugging along. So Reed pushed the dead animal in further.

More blood.

More bones crunching.

He watched as the head of the rodent disappeared deeper into the small opening. That's when he got his first look at it. The small hole in the ground had teeth. And after fully engulfing the rabbit, the mouth stretched a tad bit wider. William was perplexed—

It was a goddamn *mouth.*

Monstrous teeth in the ground, right there, smack dab in the middle of one of his forgotten acres. And we're not talking missing human or animal teeth: the ground had *an actual mouth* with two visible rows of teeth.

William kneeled to get a better look at the ground kisser. It was as bizarre and weird as can be, but it was also stunning. And it felt a bit magical, like it was something out of a fairy tale. *Or a nightmare.* He looked over the small dirty pearls with strands of bloody bunny and saliva strung between the teeth.

William Reed suddenly had something to feed. And feed it he did.

At first, he relied on local wildlife to feed the beast, but that was far too sporadic to count on. So he decided he would become the number one customer at the local pet store in town. He wouldn't buy cats or anything like that, he stuck to the mice they used to feed snakes. He figured that would be less suspicious. And even if they were suspicious, there was zero proof of anything weird out at his property. Pete at Pete's Pets didn't need to know anything about the hole in the ground. He didn't need to know anything about anything. He just needed to have a few boxes of mice ready every week.

It was strictly a transaction.

And the mice were strictly a meal for the slow growing mouth.

Reed was dumbfounded by the creature. It seemed to grow a small bit after every feeding. *How much* depended on what the teeth in the ground ate. The mice didn't have much of an impact, not like the rabbit did. There was also the fact that the teeth didn't seem to leave any proof of their meal behind. Not that Reed was pacing back and forth waiting for the teeth to take a shit, but he was oddly curious about how they digested their food. He walked a mile radius on every side of the teeth to see if there was anything at all.

There was nothing.

As far as he could tell, these teeth were a bottomless pit and if they *did* leave any gnashed up shit laying around, it had to be *far* underground, where no one would ever find it. So naturally, that realization led to bigger ideas.

About life.

About himself.

And about what else he could start feeding the teeth in the ground. Especially after reading in *The Indianapolis News* that Rand Myers would be bringing a Cyclops Pictures roadshow to the Biograph Theater in Chicago. Was a nine-hour round trip worth making Rand Myers pay for all the bullshit he had put William Reed through?

You bet your ass it was.

Rand Myers had no way of knowing he had been followed all day long.

It's hard to be aware of that sort of thing when your head is planted straight up your ass. The B-Movie mogul had just polished off his fourth bourbon of the night and made his way into the alley near the marquee. The Cyclops roadshow was an absolute bust in the city of wind, so Myers passed the time with alcohol. Lots of alcohol.

Which made him even more oblivious to his stalker. William Reed was just fine with that, though. It made things easier. There would be less struggle, and hopefully less yelling. He watched as Myers starting to make a urine design all over the old Chicago brick. Then he made his move.

Reed had been drinking as well to build his courage and had the empty proof of that very fact in his right hand. He brought the bottle down on Rand's head, knocking the poor bastard into the remnants of his own piss trail. The B-movie mogul spun around, startled by the assault and shocked by who had committed it.

"Reed?! We thought you were dead!"

William grinned.

"You're going to wish I was when this is all said and done."

William brought his boot down onto Rand's face, knocking him out cold. Reed checked his surroundings, then promptly vomited all over the same brick wall Myers had just pissed on. He had never done anything like this before. He had never even really been a violent person, yet here he was. Assaulting and kidnapping a man who did him wrong so many years ago.

He hoisted the dead weight of Myers over his shoulder so the man would appear blackout drunk. They limped out of the alley, stopping to let a group of strangers pass by. One of the passersby gave a concerned look, but Reed mimed a bottle-to-his-mouth motion. A nod of understanding, then the group kept walking.

William noticed the blood dripping from Rand's head and chuckled at the irony of this whole thing happening in front of the same theater John Dillinger died in front of. He felt a certain outlaw kinship to the whole thing. Reed took one last look at the Biograph marquee and the taunting letters of the Cyclops Pictures Roadshow.

It was time for his own roadshow to begin.

Rand Myers woke up once they were already back in Indiana. Reed could hear the furious thumping in the trunk, and his nerves returned. But he was too far gone now. Even if he had a change of heart and let the scumbag go, Myers now knew that Reed was alive, and it would only be a matter of time before he was found. So the plan remained, and he found himself more excited by it the closer he got to his seven acres of revenge.

William knew he would have to act fast once he opened the trunk. He knew that Rand would try to fight, and well, that just couldn't happen. The hole was hungry, and Reed was hungry for revenge. He popped open the latch, and sure as shit, Rand lunged for him immediately. But Reed was prepared. He let the restrained bastard topple off the edge and smash down onto the rocky driveway.

While down, William taped Rand's mouth shut, then briefly disappeared into the nearby barn. Rand attempted to use this opportunity to crawl away, but that proved pretty impossible without full use of his wrists and legs. So he lay wiggling helplessly across the ground.

"Where you off to, Prince Randian?" William asked, with a heavy dose of taunt.

Rand unleashed a muffled scream as William set down some rope, a backpack, and a full body sled. He grabbed Rand and pushed his body on top of the sled, crafting a makeshift cart moments later. Then William set out into the woods.

Every once in a while, he would look back to make sure he still had his cargo. He'd wipe the sweat from his face and keep pulling. They were getting closer to the hole in the ground. Which meant he was getting closer to a new beginning. One where the taste of failure and lies didn't exist.

Just blood and teeth in the ground.

William kneeled and stared at the wiggling man restrained on the sled. He pulled the tape off of Rand's mouth and let out a deep sigh.

"I've been waiting a long time for this."

"What the hell is wrong with you, William?"

"It's not William anymore. It's Wayne."

Wayne was proud of his new name, even if it wasn't all that exciting or original. It was the first step to reclaiming his love of the Old West. His love of John Ford. And yes, his love of The Duke himself, John Wayne. The pair did fourteen films together and as far as *Wayne Rogers* was concerned, they were all great. He grinned as he thought back to their 1940 collaboration, *The Long Voyage Home*, the film that cinematographer Gregg Toland had masterfully shot before shooting *Citizen Kane* the very next year. *Voyage* was a movie where The Duke didn't speak much, and Wayne felt exceptionally connected to it at the current moment. He himself had been on a long voyage home and he didn't need to say much at all.

"It doesn't matter what your name is, kid. They'll find out about all of this."

Wayne pulled Rand's helpless body off the sled and let out a small laugh.

"I have a new friend that says otherwise."

The confused Rand followed Will—Wayne's eyes to a small hole in the ground. The mouth was now the size of a decent salad bowl. It was being fed well and it knew it was once again feeding time. Rand grew frantic as Wayne pulled him closer.

"Look, we'll make your movie. What was it? *The Guy from Wyoming*? We'll do it!"

Wayne let out a laugh and shook his head in embarrassment.

"You think I'm still interested in that? In making your little movies? No, no, no. *This* is all for me now, Rand."

Wayne pulled out a Sony 8mm Handycam and a tripod. He set the equipment up so it could fully focus on Rand and the hole. He pressed down on the record button.

"But don't get me wrong, I'm still interested in creating something for you."

"Anything! What is it?" The desperate Rand cried out.

"Pain."

Wayne smiled, then once again covered Rand's mouth with tape. He pulled the body closer to the teeth in the ground.

"You killed my dream, Rand. And you stole my life. So now . . . we steal yours."

Wayne flipped the sled, knocking Rand face-first right up against the hole in the ground. Muffled screams spilled out from behind the tape. Wayne ignored him and walked over to check the framing of the footage. A slight adjustment on the camera, then he returned and focused *only* on the teeth.

"I hope you're hungry. You're eating *good* tonight."

Wayne lifted Rand's tied ankles and placed them inside the hole. It didn't take long for the feast to begin. Just like feeding a pencil into a sharpener, Wayne guided Rand's helpless body as the hole continued to eat.

He was pleased by the muffled screams and disappointed by the lack of blood spray but there was simply no space for it to escape. Rand's body was too big, and the teeth were just too small . . . for the time being. The teeth in the ground were growing with every single bite. And they rumbled with joy at the taste of the poor bastard being slowly devoured.

Wayne grinned as he shoved Rand into the hole up to his abdomen. The sleazy fucker was still begging for Wayne to change his mind but it was far too late for that. Besides, Rand wasn't going to survive much longer. He'd be dead way before his head reached the hole. Wayne decided he'd take the tape off and give the slimy bastard some final words.

Rand eyed Wayne not with anger, but with shame. He spit out a chunk of bloody gore and let out what would be his final laugh.

"You never had what it takes. You never will. You're always going to be a hack. And that's what they'll remember you for, William. Being . . . a . . . hack."

Wayne growled and placed his hands on top of Rand's bleeding, sweaty head.

"It's Wayne Rogers now."

He shoved Rand Myers deep into the ground with all his might and finally got the blood spray he had so desperately wanted. A few moments later, Rand Myers was no more. And the hole had grown even bigger.

Wayne wiped a swath of blood away from his face and stared out in front of him. He wasn't worried about the mess or any of the struggles he had with Rand. He knew it would be much easier next time. And oh yes, there would *definitely* be a next time. And many more after that. Because the teeth in the ground now had the taste.

And so did Wayne Rogers.

DILLSBORO DISCOVERY

RUSTY STILL COULDN'T believe his eyes.

The small room in his new basement was filled to the brim with videotapes, movie memorabilia, and a TV set with a VCR still connected to it. There were loads of old VHS tapes lined up on a shelf. It was like they stumbled into the backroom of a secret swap meet. A clearly disappointed Abigail investigated each case by shouting out whatever was written on the side of it.

"This one says *Paul*. The tape next to it says *Cherry Pike*," She plucked another one from the shelf and held it up for Rusty to see. "But this one just says *Coyote*. What do you suppose that means?"

Rusty stared back in silence. He had no idea what it meant. He didn't know what any of this meant. He took a step closer to an old poster on the wall. A creased ad for an old movie called *Brontosaurus Babylonia*, and the art had different variations of the Brontosaurus on it. Some were in clothes, others had hats. It was absolutely ridiculous.

"Rust?" Abigail called out. He turned to see her still holding the coyote tape up. "Any guesses?"

He shook his head and went back to the movie poster. She joined him at his art museum gaze in front of *Brontosaurus Babylonia*, sizing up the weird little dinosaurs. "Holy shit. I forgot about this movie."

"It's a real movie?" he asked, trying to wrap his head around dinosaurs in clothes.

She gave an over-exaggerated nod. "Yeah, dude. It's old and so awful. But it *is* a movie. Fun fact, this predates *Tammy and the T-Rex* by like twenty years."

He delivered his trademark confused face.

"*Tammy and the T-Rex*. Dude, come on. An evil scientist sticks Paul Walker's brain into—"

Rusty didn't care at all. "Why's it down here?"

Abigail leaned in closer to the poster. "*Directed by William Reed*. Never heard of him. Have you?" Rusty shook his head.

Abigail looked at the other wall, another movie poster. A large ball of hair was on the front, terrorizing a small sleepy town. "*Hair*

Ball." She cleared her throat and put on her best movie trailer voice. "*Welcome to Pacific City . . . where things are about to get hairy.* Jesus Christ. Who made this shit?" She leaned in closer to the credit block on the poster. "Fuckin' A . . . William Reed."

They both looked around at the rest of the old movie memorabilia. "It's all William Reed," Rusty said, as if he was shouting out clues to Sherlock Holmes. Her face shrunk.

"It's like a shrine to some shitty filmmaker. No wonder he kept it all hidden. This is just embarrassing. I'm just so—" She made a *blah* sound and sighed in disappointment. She picked up two cheap looking ghost masks. "These are fucking cool though!"

She flipped them over to see *Cycle Ghouls* prop masks written in marker.

Rusty walked over to the shelf of videotapes. He pulled off the hard case for *Brontosaurus Babylonia* and went straight for the VHS player.

"You don't want to do that, man. It has a Brontosaurus riding on an actual oversized skateboard. It's just so BAD."

Rusty ignored her, partially because he was intrigued by the idea of a dinosaur on a skateboard but mostly because he wanted to find out more about the William Reed character. And just what the hell Wayne found so important about the guy.

Abigail turned her attention back to the shelf of movies. "Too bad he didn't own any of the good old school horror shit on tape. Like the three C's."

Rusty turned back toward her. "Three C's?"

"Carpenter, Craven, and Cronenberg. The holy trinity of horror." She moved her hand across her body like she was paying tribute to the Father, the Son, and the Holy Spirit. Then, she quickly dropped the act and went back to the VHS spines. "Bet you didn't know that Cronenberg technically had the last real VHS release, did you?"

Rusty shook his head. He did *not* know that.

"It's true. And it wasn't even like pure Cronenbergian goodness. It was the one with the sixty-nine in it."

Rusty let out a shocked cough and turned to her. She nodded. *Yeah, dude. Sixty-nine.*

"Pure oral copulation. Just Aragon and Coyote Ugly on a tongue trip downtown together. Think about it. Cronenberg didn't even have sixty-nine in *Crash* and that's *crazy* since the whole point of that movie is doing weird sex shit in crashed cars. Which speaking of, man, I was way too young when I watched James Spader have sex with a thigh scar. That might actually explain some shit up top." She pointed to her head and laughed.

Rusty did not laugh.

He made a sound that basically said *I'm super uncomfortable so I'm going to act like this whole exchange didn't just happen.* He turned back to the VHS player and pushed *Brontosaurus Babylonia* into the slot . . . but there was already something in there. He hit the eject button and pulled out the VHS tape that had been living inside the device.

He stared down at the cassette in his hands.

"Let me guess, *Plan 9 From Outer Space*?" Abigail said with the confidence of a stand-up comedian. Rusty shook his head and turned to face her. He lifted the tape up so she could easily read the taped-on label.

"Holy shit."

Holy shit, indeed.

Rusty spun the tape back in front of him and reread the label, just to make sure his eyes weren't tricking him. They weren't. The VHS tape had three words written on it in black ink:

Play me, Rusty.

On the videotape, Wayne stood by the clearing in the woods.

Rusty and Abigail could tell he was near Mouth, but still a bit away. He looked tired and beat down. He coughed occasionally and would have to stop and wipe his cheeks free of whatever phlegm landed there. Rusty gathered that this tape had to have been made after their lunch together.

"*Hey Rusty, I don't know exactly how long it took you to find this tape. Or if it's even you that's watching it. Maybe you're long dead and this property now belongs to somebody else. Or maybe . . . he got out. What a shit show that would be. Hopefully it's still you and still just your eyes only.*"

Rusty paused the tape and looked over at Abigail. "Maybe you should—"

She cut him off. "Hell no. You wouldn't have even found this without my help. I'm staying put." He sighed and pressed play again.

"You're probably a little confused by all of this. It's funny to think that you've been taking care of our friend Mouth, yet all the bullshit in that room is where things start to get . . . weird. We'll come back to all of that. First, let's talk about Mouth. Him and I, we have formed quite the bond over the last thirty or so years. Shit, so much so, the thought of all of this makes me, well . . ."

Wayne wiped his eyes and looked off screen. He focused back on the camera.

"You know, I didn't even want to name him at first. But he belonged to me, so I figured I should probably call him something other than the big ole fucking weirdo thing I had been calling it. Not out of disrespect or anything. He is an actual mouth IN the ground. In my eyes, even Webster's dictionary would define that as a big ole fucking weirdo thing. I called him 'teeth in the ground' for a few months but that didn't fit either. One day I just called him Mouth and it seemed to stick. That's what he's been called ever since."

Rusty looked over at Abigail, who unleashed a mocking round of applause.

"Brilliant. He decided to call the mouth . . . Mouth."

Rusty focused back on the video.

"I'm telling you all of that so you know I cared about him. Still care about him. And he cared about me. We were companions."

Abigail unleashed a loud *holy shit* groan that pulled Rusty away from the video.

"What?!"

"He said they were companions. Do you think he would like, lay down or hover over the—"

Rusty cut her off. "Please stop."

"Back to the room you're in now. Some of those tapes and posters . . . they're from a different life. Other tapes, those are from this life. One with a hungry Mouth." He coughed and wiped his lips. *"I'm sure you're wondering who William Reed is. Well, it's me. I'm William Reed."*

Abigail smacked Rusty on the arm. "Holy shit, dude. *The William Reed.*" She made a fart noise and sunk back into her chair as Wayne-slash-William continued.

"I used to make movies, if you can even call them that. They were low budget shlock, and I hated every minute of it. I never wanted to be that person. Hell, I never wanted to be this person, the one that had lunch with you. The one that's talking to you right now. But life has a funny way of altering our plans. It has a funny way of fucking everything up. It also has a funny way of bringing misfits together—"

Rusty and Abigail shared a brief look, then shifted their focus back to the TV.

"That's where you come in, Rusty. I told you two important things over lunch. That I was sick and would be dead within the week. That bit is true. By the time you see this, I've been at the bottom of Mouth since the day we had lunch."

Rusty and Abigail shared a look that screamed *what the fuck.*

"The other thing I said is that I could see myself in you. You probably took that as a bit of a compliment. Something a nice old man would say to lift the spirits of a poor drifter. But that's not what I meant. I'm a bad person and I've been a bad person ever since I left California. Hell, even before I left California. I think some of the locals have a nickname for me around here—"

Abigail looked over at Rusty, eyes as big as can be. "Dillsboro Death Dealer." Another cough from Video Wayne.

"I told you that Mouth had a very specific diet . . . and that you'd have to keep up on it. I didn't just mean the mice, Rusty. I meant everything. I meant people." Another shared look between Rusty and Abigail as the tape continued. *"The first person Mouth ever ate was named Rand Myers. It's on a tape down here somewhere. I won't bore you with the miserable facts of his life, but he deserved every bite he got. When it was all over, I could tell that Mouth wanted more just by the way the ground shook. I could feel his rage and hunger under my feet. He never let me stop after that moment. So, he'd get that special treat one day a week. And I kept that up until now. Hitchhikers, addicts, criminals, and more. They've all been to the bottom of the teeth in the ground. And there are the tapes to prove it."*

Rusty stared at the television screen in horror. Abigail mostly in fascinating shock.

"So now . . . that brings us to your current situation. You're now responsible for Mouth, which means you are now

responsible for everything, including that special treat. There's no way out of it, Rusty. Believe me. I tried to stop once and Mouth . . . he didn't like it much. It felt like he was trying to tear himself out of the ground. Maybe to get at me. Maybe to get at the world. Maybe both. Seems like that's sort of how things go with things like us. There's always something after us. Our past. Our misery. Our hunger. Either way, we went back to that diet pretty quickly. And we've been that way ever since. You're probably cussing me right now, but I want you to know: I used to feed him people like you. We met each other at the perfect time, Rusty. Now I'm at the bottom of the teeth in the ground and you're me. Stick to the people who won't be missed. Believe me. It makes it all so much easier."

Then, Wayne waved at the camera and turned the camcorder off. The TV screen went blank, allowing Abigail to see Rusty's pale face in the reflection. She could sense the weight of the monstrous agreement weighing on his shoulders. He slowly looked over, trying to find the words, but she beat him to the punch—

"You better not even be thinking about feeding me to that fucking thing!"

"It was like they had stumbled into the backroom of a secret swap meet."

MOUTH CURSE

ABIGAIL KEPT HER eyes locked on Rusty.

They clomped through the woods, heading out to pay the man-eating Mouth a visit. She wanted to hold up the small camcorder she "borrowed" from the Reed collection and record Rusty in what appeared to be a vulnerable moment. He was carrying another box of mice, grumbling to himself. His eyes looked like they were fluctuating between being on the verge of tears and an angry meltdown.

She wondered what he was thinking about with such visible frustration. That answer should have been painfully obvious at this point. Old man Wayne left him with a curse. But she knew it had to be more than that.

Was it her? Was it the camera? Was she an added stress on his life now?

"What are you thinking about?" she asked, hoping to pry a small conversation out of the trip. He looked at her, then shook his head, continuing the path forward. "Are you mad at Wayne . . . or William?" She raised the camcorder and looked through the lens. "Speaking of, *this* is a great time to talk about it. What are we calling him at this point? I mean, the dude has so many names, but you know my vote. The Dillsbo—"

"Not that."

"Okay. I mean, that's one of his names though. And it's a particularly good one. It carries a certain . . . bravado." She stopped and looked around at the swaying trees. "Dude, think about it. You probably have ghosts." She raised the camcorder and watched the trees through the camera. She liked the way the lens made the world look. She turned back to Rusty, who hadn't even acknowledged the comment, so she kept at it—

"Have you heard of Herb Baumeister? Your property might be giving him a run for his money." He still ignored her. "He lived up North. The guy killed like twenty-five men and burned the bodies, pulverized the bones, and buried them all over his property. They're still finding victims to *this* day. There are *definitely* fucking ghosts on *that* property."

"I don't believe in ghosts." Rusty muttered from under his breath. Abigail looked over in shock. *He lives!*

"What do you mean you don't believe in ghosts? How is that even possible?"

"Never believed in 'em. Too far-fetched." He shrugged, adjusting the box of popcorn mice. Abigail stopped in her tracks.

"Ghosts are too far-fetched? Yet we're on our way to feed a living mouth in the ground." Rusty stopped and looked back at her.

"*I'm* on my way to feed the mouth—listen, don't you have to go to work or something?"

"No. They fired me for leaving my shift the other day. So, I'm free to help." Rusty took off walking again, shaking his head in a *that's-what-you-get-for-following-me* sort of way.

"Don't you want another job?" he asked, trying to scratch an itch on his chin with the corner of the box.

"Not really. They kind of take up all your time. And I think I'm just going to go with the flow like you do. Maybe some murderous old man will leave me his death house someday!"

Rusty shook his head. "What are you going to do for money?"

She grinned. "I have some ideas."

He stopped walking again and shot her a look. She was holding the camera up for him to see as clear as day. *What the hell is that supposed to mean?* But before he could ask, a horrendous and haunting scream rang out in the distance. They both looked in the same direction.

"Fuck! Ghosts!" Abigail excitedly screamed and pushed down on the record button.

But it wasn't even close to being a bogey or a ghoul. They were both shocked at what was actually screaming out in horror. A massive white-tailed deer had fallen inside Mouth and was being devoured at a very slow, painful pace.

Abigail and Rusty stood and watched awkwardly as the deer pawed and tried to use its antlers to escape, but it was no use. The animal was sucked deeper and deeper in. Abigail slowly raised the camera and focused in on the poor deer. Then, she put on an old timey radio voice—

"And the latest production from director William Reed . . . *Bambi Versus the Teeth in the Ground!*"

Rusty tried his best not to vomit . . . but that was easier said than done.

The antlers of the deer were stuck in the corner of Mouth's, well, mouth. So he had to carefully pluck the remaining chunk of the animal out from the horrific teeth . . . the remaining chunk being the top half of the deer head still attached to the antlers.

There was also the challenging fact that a piece of antler had somehow gotten lodged in between some of the teeth. Rusty figured it had snapped off when the deer was using every ounce of itself to try to get out. He had no idea how he was going to get the piece free without losing a piece of himself.

"Hold tight, Mouth. I'll get this figured out," Rusty said, scratching his head at the current situation. He turned to see Abigail crouched on the ground, getting an extreme closeup of what remained of the deer. "Are you actually recording all this?!"

She pulled the camcorder back and jumped up on her feet. "I'm just messing around with this thing. Plus, that's a cool shot, dude. It's like a real horror prop."

He shook his head, annoyed by the conversation. "No, it's not like a *real horror prop*. That was a living thing a few minutes ago. Show a little bit of compassion."

Abigail shrugged and dropped the camera to her side. "Sorry, man." She slowly approached Rusty and Mouth and stared down at the chunk of the antler that was giving Mouth hell. "How you going to get that out of there?"

"No idea. I can't really call a dentist."

"I mean, you could. You'd just have to feed 'em to Mouth after," Abigail said, with a massive grin.

"That's not happening."

"Then what's the plan, Doc?"

Rusty let out a deep sigh and removed his hat from his sweaty head. He scratched the hat hair and put the cap back on. He paced around, his eyes darting from the deer remains to the big hole in the ground.

"I think I saw some rope and shovels in the barn."

"Okay?" Abigail said, clearly confused by the statement. "What's that mean?"

Rusty shook his head and kneeled to get a closer look at the antler chunk. He didn't know what any of this meant anymore. Just one *can you believe this shit* after another. He was still trying to process the fact that he was conned into taking over the Mouth operation from a murderous old man. He was still trying to adjust to having Abigail's never ending energy and her constant yapping in his ear. And now . . . he had this deer situation to worry about. It was the current tip of the *can you believe this shit* iceberg.

"Well, if I can't get a dentist out here . . . I guess I need to become one."

They both looked down into Mouth. Abigail's face lit up.

"Oh, I'm definitely getting that on camera."

BAMBI VERSUS THE TEETH IN THE GROUND

MOUTH HAD NEVER felt anything like that before.

Up until now, almost all the special treats went down so easy. Sure, they would make noises and move around, but the teeth did their job. The choppers made sure there were no more noises. No more movement. He liked it when they stopped moving.

He liked the way they tasted. He *oh so loved* these special treats! They brought him happiness and made him feel . . . complete. Like that's what he was put here for.

To feast on these . . . things.

But something was different about this new morsel. It wasn't the same at all. And even worse, it did *not* want to be eaten. So much so, it was fighting back!

Nothing had ever done that before . . . and it hurt?

It kept jabbing the sides of him and kicking.

Oh, the kicking! That didn't feel good at all!

But . . . it finally went down. Almost all of it. And then it left a piece of itself, and the teeth couldn't get to it. Mouth could feel the chunk stabbing into the side of him. He wanted to cry. He wanted to shake. He wanted to—

"Now Mouth . . . I'm going to try and get the piece of antler out. So please don't shake the ground. Or eat me. That's the most important thing."

Mouth focused all his attention on his friend Rusty. *He wanted to help!* And sure, he said "don't shake," but Mouth was determined to show his appreciation . . . and sense of humor. So, he shook the ground just a touch. His friend shook with it.

"What did I just say?!?"

Mouth wanted to shake the ground again, to let his friend know he was just messing around. But he chose to listen this time. Plus, he didn't want to delay whatever help Rusty was offering. And he didn't know exactly what that plan was, but he would remain as still as could be until it was over.

Then, Rusty suddenly whacked his tooth with the sharp end of something. The pain returned, causing Mouth to shake with rage.

And for the first time ever, he felt like swallowing his new friend whole.

TEETH
CLEAN

ABIGAIL FOCUSED HER newly claimed camcorder directly on Rusty.

He carefully held the blade of the shovel above the antler-stuffed section of Mouth's teeth. She could tell his nerves were getting the best of him. But the camera was getting so much more. She watched as he nervously placed his feet over the gap. It would be one hell of a show if he happened to fall in while trying to help his pet monster. Abigail zoomed in as he took another step closer to the edge.

"Now Mouth . . . I'm going to try to get the piece of antler out. So please don't shake the ground. Or eat me. That's the most important thing."

The ground shook a little and the small rumble was enough to jolt Rusty's nerves. "What did I just say?!" The ground stopped shaking. Abigail grinned as Rusty turned and glared at her and the camera. "Oh, I bet you just loved that!"

"It was *pretty* great. You got to love a hole with a personality!"

Rusty shook his head and refocused his attention on the teeth and the blade of the shovel. Abigail lowered the camera and called out just as he started to make a move—

"Do you think he can sing?"

"What?" He looked over at her, still holding the shovel above the tainted area.

"Mouth. Do you think he can sing? You know, like Audrey 2."

"He can't even talk. How would he be able to sing?"

Abigail looked over the ground and the massive hole. "He talks. He just does it with movement. Like subterranean sign language. I bet his singing has more movement."

"Well, maybe we don't encourage that sort of thing when I'm standing directly over him!"

Abigail nodded. *Good point.*

"Roger that." She raised the camera and zoomed in on Rusty trying to fine tune his approach. Then she started to sing. "*He's got your number now—*"

Rusty turned and shook his head. "*Abigail!*"

"*Little Shop*, dude."

"I know that! But can we maybe not sing or make any sort of noise right now?" Abigail nodded and delivered an apologetic face. Rusty turned back to Mouth and used the tip of the shovel to touch the chunk of antler.

It didn't move a bit.

He delivered a more forceful hit. The impact loosened it a little, but it also hurt Mouth. The ground shook in shocked reaction, jostling Rusty around.

"Whoa, whoa. Easy now."

The ground slowed back to being perfectly still. Rusty looked back at Abigail. She raised her free hand and delivered a *you got this* thumbs up. Her face hidden behind the camera said, *you are going to die.*

He used the shovel a few more times with varying degrees of success. He put his hands on his hips Alan Grant-style and looked at Abigail.

"It's still stuck."

"So, what now?"

Rusty turned and went to his pile of random tools and supplies on the ground. She watched as he picked up a hoe and tied one end of the rope closest to the blade. He grabbed another tool with a similar bladed edge and walked over to Mouth. Abigail was fascinated by his tool concoction.

She focused the camera as Rusty hung the loose end of the rope into Mouth, doing his best to fisherman the rope in between the teeth. It took a few attempts, but he managed to place it in the perfect spot. He used the other tool to scoop up the loose, hanging end of the rope. Then, he tied it to the end of the new tool. He took a step back and turned to Abigail—

"Going to need your help on this one, Hitchcock."

She lowered the camera and glared. "Of all the filmmakers in the world. Of all the filmmakers in general. Of all the filmmakers we've talked about, that's the one you chose to call me?"

"Would you have preferred someone else?"

"Other than that abusive hate monger? No, I can't really think of anyone in particular."

Rusty laughed and put his hands on his hips. "Really? I'm shocked."

Abigail took a hard swallow and a deep breath—

"Spielberg. Carpenter. Peele. Lynch. Heckerling. Coppola. *The other Coppola*. Craven. Talalay. Romero. Cronenberg. *The other Cronenberg*. Kusama. Derrickson. Alvarez. Ephron. Fincher. Aster. Harron. Burton. Reichardt. Del Toro. Soderbergh. Gerwig. Miller. Ramsay. Tarantino. Fucking Scorsese. Bigelow. Raimi. Waititi. Ducournau. Smith. Flanagan. McKend—"

"Okay, okay!" Rusty shook his head and laughed. "Did you want me to call you all of those people??"

Abigail took a breath and set the camera down. "What do you need me to do?"

He eyed one of the tools attached to the rope. "Need you to pull that side. We're going to do it like a canoe paddle. Or a saw. Back and forth."

Abigail sighed, trying her damnedest to hide the disappointment of not getting something like that recorded. She picked up her tool and looked down into the hole. The rope was a massive line of floss. She grinned across the opening at Rusty.

"Never in a million years did I think I'd be doing something like this."

He nodded. "That makes two of us." Then, he gave the go ahead for her to start. She pulled her end, then Rusty pulled back on his. They went about this scenario for a few minutes until the antler piece was suddenly dislodged by the two-person floss team.

The chunk fell deep into Mouth. Abigail watched as Rusty walked over to what remained of the deer head and snapped the antlers off, leaving the remains in three pieces. He dropped each piece into the grateful and now pain-free Mouth.

Abigail picked up the camera and started recording again just as Rusty picked up a deck brush. He stood over the teeth in the ground—

"Almost done, Mouth. Just need to give you a slight scrub." He looked at the bristly end of the brush. "This might tickle a bit." He lowered the tool into the mouth and scrubbed the area impacted by the piece of the antler.

She laughed at the heartwarming sight of a grinning Rusty brushing the monstrous teeth. And the uncontrollable quivering the ground was doing. It was quite the scene. Rusty looked over at the camera, like a zookeeper tending to an elephant.

"I haven't been this happy in years," he said, smiling from ear to ear. "I wish people could see this."

Abigail wished for the same thing.

In fact, it was the whole reason she took the camcorder in the first place. She wanted the world to meet Mouth, but not as a monstrous thing. She wanted the world to know the sweet, hungry teeth in the ground. The one that would laugh and play around with people. No, to her and the camera, Mouth wasn't a monster. He was a star.

And she was ready to give him his close-up.

ABIGAIL
THE
GOBY

ABIGAIL **LOOKED OUT** at her bedroom walls.

They were filled with makeshift dreamcatchers, beads, and old, taped up movie posters. The selection was mostly horror, but there were some other genres sprinkled in. That wasn't her choice, though. She bought a massive bundle of used posters from someone who claimed to be an old video store clerk on eBay. They also claimed the bundle was entirely horror.

The seller was entirely wrong.

A few of the posters were absolute duds like *Wild Wild West, Speed 2: Cruise Control, Chairman of the Board* (yes, the *Carrot Top surfing in an office* poster) and *Blank Check*. There was also a ripped up *Dazed and Confused* and a faded *Trainspotting*. Luckily for her, the *not-* entirely bundle of horror posters had some horrific gold in it. She lucked out with *Scream, From Dusk Til Dawn, The Faculty, Army of Darkness, Arachnophobia, Halloween H2O, Sleepy Hollow, Event Horizon, Misery, Tremors,* and *The Blair Witch Project*.

Not bad for a little more than $25.

Bad if you only had a limited amount of decorating space in your tiny duplex bedroom.

And that was Abigail. Her choices were limited, so she went with *The Faculty, Army of Darkness, Tremors,* and *The Blair Witch Project*. She also hung the *Blank Check* poster in the hopes that someone would one day write her a blank check to make a horror movie like the ones on her wall. But she crossed out the word Disney and wrote the word "Gimme" in the Disney font.

Gimme Blank Check.

She laughed every time she walked by it. Or every time she thought about it. But right now, she was only thinking about two of the posters hanging on her off-white walls: *Tremors* and *The Blair Witch Project*. She stared out at the terrified face of Heather Donahue and thought about how the poster design *sort of* resembled a mouth in the woods.

Or maybe that's just because she was so used to seeing an *actual* Mouth in the woods.

She eyed the *Tremors* poster. That design teased a monstrous Graboid underground, mouth open under the feet of the three stars of the movie. Then, she looked at the stack of videotapes piled up on her bed.

"Rusty's going to kill me," she thought out loud.

She wondered if he had realized she went back inside the house when he was still finishing up with Mouth's dental work. Or if he had even noticed that she raided half of Wayne-slash-William's stash of found footage snuff films. Would he be mad, or would he be fine with her watching them?

That was *if* she were *just* planning on watching them.

That would imply that she didn't have an RCA cable currently connecting her VCR player to the back of her laptop. Or new digitizing software downloading. That would also imply that she had zero plans for Wayne-slash-William's footage or for the footage she had been filming on Wayne-slash-William's old camcorder the last few days.

That would also imply that she hadn't gone out of her way to send a message to a local scumbag named Carson. She laughed at that thought in particular. Going out of your way was like . . . going a few extra miles to take a friend home or to try out a new hip restaurant. It wasn't doing your makeup and taking a sexy selfie. It wasn't sending said sexy selfie to a known creep with a message to meet you in the woods to make a little movie.

That's not going out of the way. That's being out of your fucking mind.

And maybe she was.

Abigail hadn't done much with the nineteen years of her life up to this point. She'd been bullied and beaten and had run away from it all. She had a miserable, dead-end job at Paul's Pets. And she always had a desire to make movies. Now, she was unemployed and had already paid her rent and bills for the month. She figured she could hide out in her tiny apartment for another week or two until Rusty got suspicious.

Luckily for her, she never told him where she lived. She never told *anyone* where she lived. Definitely not creepy Carson. That was just part of her old habit of never trusting anyone mixed with that whole *running away from life* thing. She was sure she had people out there looking for her. Bill collectors, definitely Bob the

Principal, a few ex-boyfriends and girlfriends, her mom, and now probably Rusty.

Well, maybe not Rusty.

He didn't seem like the others. Not violent or angry all the time. He seemed different, like he just wanted to be left alone, or at least left in silence. She realized she never asked him what his story was. How he ended up roaming the roads of America or how he even ended up down in Dillsboro.

On the other hand, she never really told him much about herself, either. Sure, he seemed annoyed by her and tried his best to get rid of her. *His* style, not Wayne style . . . thankfully. There was a small part of her that felt like he didn't mind having her around, like she was filling in a missing piece of himself.

She wondered what piece that was. And if he would ever get it back.

Abigail thought back on an old nature documentary she watched that was about mutualism and the symbiotic relationships different species form together for the benefit of both. She smiled at the thought of her and Rusty having a symbiotic relationship.

Like the pistol shrimp and gobies.

The shrimp were the burrowers that would share their holes with a goby. Once outside of the area, the pair would stay close together. If danger came around, the pair would use each other for safety. Then, the goby would always be the first one to venture back out. And the shrimp would then follow.

A true symbiotic relationship that shared a hole.

In this situation, Mouth was the obvious hole burrowed in the ocean floor. But she wondered if she was the shrimp or the goby? So far, it seemed as if she was the goby of the pair. Rusty always seemed nervous and afraid. Like whatever was out there was going to hurt him. Or upset him.

And she understood that feeling.

But she was the one that took charge and helped him find Wayne-slash-William's secret snuff room. And she was the one that could tell something was up with all the mice orders which, in turn, had led her out to Mouth.

And again, Rusty hadn't asked her to leave. He had just accepted her like it was a benefit to him for her to be around.

So, she figured she was the goby.

And Rusty was the pistol shrimp.

The only thing left to figure out was what kind of mutualism this situation was. The one where they were entirely dependent on each other or the one where the benefits help, but they can survive without each other.

Abigail figured that question, and others, would be answered when she finished watching all of Wayne-slash-William's footage she had borrowed and started working on her new idea. She didn't know exactly how she was going to get there, but she knew the road she wanted to take.

As she waited for the files to upload, she clicked on a folder labeled *Rusty*. She double clicked a file called "Teeth Clean" and watched as Rusty brushed the teeth of Mouth. She grinned as the recorded version of Rusty smiled. He looked over at the camera—

"I wish people could see this."

That was her new goal in life. For people to see *this*. To see Rusty caring for Mouth. To see Mouth in general. And to see the work of Wayne-slash-William-slash-the Dillsboro Death Dealer. She wanted the world to know that monsters *did* exist. But that they weren't like we imagined them or like the ones on her walls.

They weren't Deadites. They weren't aliens invading a high school. They weren't dirt dragons or a witch in the woods. And they certainly weren't the teeth in the ground. They were the people we knew or the people we thought we knew. She wanted to show the world what a monster really looked like. And she was going to start doing that as soon as the footage uploaded.

It was time for the goby to see if the shrimp would follow her lead.

SHRIMP
AND
GRIT

RUSTY STARED AT the ransacked shelves.

He hadn't been down in the hidden basement room since the day they discovered it. He also hadn't seen Abigail since Mouth's makeshift dental appointment. And while the silence and reclaimed solitude was nice, the situation was starting to make him very uncomfortable.

For one, he sort of liked having her around.

She had broken up his mundane life of ambling around in silence. Mouth had done that as well, but he couldn't quite carry a conversation without nearly shaking someone inside his hole. So, Abigail provided a safety net of discussion. Even if he didn't know or care what the hell she was rambling on about most of the time.

He would occasionally chuckle to himself about the film related rants she would go on. Sure, she was loud and abrasive, but she knew things that he didn't. That was always helpful when you have spent the last ten or so years alone and disconnected from the world.

That happened when your whole life fell apart.

But . . . he also didn't know her very well. She followed him home from the pet store because she didn't believe him. She knew specific details about Mouth and his unnatural diet. Mouth was enough to stress out about, but knowing that he had eaten people? And on top of that, knowing the truth about the person who had fed Mouth said people?

It was all shaping up to be a recipe for disaster.

He felt like he should go upstairs and watch for the cops or the FBI to pull in at any moment. Or he should pack what little belongings he had and hit the road in the rusty old truck Wayne *or whatever the hell his real name was* left for him.

But then what about Mouth?

He realized this was now the same predicament that Wayne *or whatever the hell his real name was* had to think about when he was making his suicide plans. What if Mouth had no one to feed him? What if what Wayne said was true . . . and Mouth would pull himself out of the ground to feed. What did he even look like?! The thought alone sent shivers down Rusty's spine.

He shook the terrifying thought away, needing to focus on the now. What if the cops or the FBI *do* come, and they bring a bunch of scientists or whatever to do tests on his buried friend? He couldn't take the risk of that happening. He wanted to help Mouth and keep him safe. Maybe that was crazy and reckless. Or maybe it was the best thing to do when you failed to protect everything else in your life.

Rusty decided that the best plan of action would be to cover Mouth up as best he could. Maybe he'd use a tarp or a piece of plywood, or he could use nature itself to hide him. And he could just move all the basement riffraff around to cover the hidden room even more. Sure, Abigail would know where the door was, but maybe she wouldn't escort Johnny Law on the investigation.

Maybe they would just be acting on a tip.

"Hi, sir. We heard you were hiding a subterranean teeth beast on the grounds that happens to have a considerable appetite for human flesh. Can we come in and check that out?"

The thought alone was ridiculous, but he was used to the ridiculous happening to him.

He took one last look at the interior of Wayne's hidden room and closed it up. He moved the piano to the other side of the basement and slid over a heavy, wooden bookcase. He filled the shelves with a bunch of random belongings. Then, he began to stack and rearrange all the boxes. An hour and a half of sweaty labor later and the room was back to being a complete mystery. He smiled at a job well done, then eyed a big tarp in the corner.

It was Mouth's turn to play hide and seek.

Rusty tried his best to control the tarp, but the Fall wind was doing its best to claim it.

He crumpled it up into a ball and held it tight against his chest as he made his way out to Mouth. If he had been thinking properly, he would have brought a box of mice to give his friend a little snack. He was starting to get nervous about what Wayne *or whatever the hell is real name is* had said about Mouth's eating habit.

Mouth was used to eating people; and if he didn't get them . . . well, Mouth got angry.

Rusty was curious as to what an angry Mouth looked like.

Would he just growl and gnash his teeth? Would Mouth suddenly learn how to use words and spew every cuss word under the sun at Rusty until Rusty fed him a random stranger?

Or was it something else?

Something worse?

He thought about what Wayne had said in the video he had left. Mouth seemed like he was trying to tear himself out of the ground to get to the world. He once again shivered at the thought.

He had no intentions of becoming the Dillsboro Death Dealer 2.0. He didn't like people, but he didn't want to feed them to Mouth just because someone else had. What a fucked up thing *that* was to ask. It'd be like babysitting a cannibal toddler whose parents kept feeding him people and you just wanted to give him a slice of pepperoni pizza.

No. Thanks.

Habits and diets could be changed. People could change. So why couldn't Mouth? Well, he wouldn't have the option. He had no choice but to change!

The people-eating days were over on this property.

Rusty adjusted the balled up tarp and pushed through the small bit of brush that led directly to Mouth. He was shocked to see a stranger standing near his friend in the ground. Rusty didn't know how to react, so he did the only thing he could think of—

"Hi?"

He grunted to himself in quiet frustration. What kind of thing is that to say to someone standing over Mouth. It should have been something like—

"Who the hell are you?" The young man said, staring back at Rusty suspiciously.

"I'm . . . Rusty."

"I don't know a Rusty. Why you here?"

Rusty took a deep gulp of nervous saliva. "I live here?"

"So . . . is she your daughter or something?"

Rusty stared back at the young man. *Daughter?*

"Well, is she?"

Rusty looked over at his wardrobe. Hoodie sweatshirt, beanie, and a stringy goatee. "Who?"

"The girl who sent me the video."

Rusty thought back on the secret snuff film room. *Shit*. He looked down at the ball of tarp and set it down on the ground. "Who are you exactly?"

"Look, I'm only here for the girl. Not whatever *this* is."

Rusty took a few steps closer to the life-sized hoodie and tightened his cheeks. "And what is *this* exactly?"

The kid was suddenly intimidated by Rusty's new fatherly approach . . . and totally unaware that he was getting closer and closer to the edge of Mouth. "Look, man. I was just told to be here. She sent a message."

"What kind of message?"

The kid pulled his phone out and cleared his throat—

"Hey Carson, my friend Vanessa told me I was your type. Wanna meet me up here and make a movie?" Carson held his phone out closer to Rusty so he could see the message, along with the sexy selfie. It was Abigail. "Do you know her?"

He wanted to shout *Not that version!* but he kept his reactions at bay. "I don't think so . . . " Rusty looked the young kid over again. "That's all it took to get you out here?"

Carson let out a small giggle and smacked his lips. "She wanted to make a movie."

Rusty shook his head. He wanted to deliver *all* the emotions. The loud, frustrated sigh. The Daniel Stern type overreaction. The violence. He wanted to cry. Rusty wanted to do all the things but instead he just said—

"You should be more careful."

Carson nodded and put his phone away. "Bet."

Rusty nodded and returned the statement. "Yep. Bet."

The kid sized Rusty up then turned to scope out the other side of the woods. "So, you live here?" He followed the tree line, down to the ground, and that's when his eyes landed on Mouth. "Yo! What the hell is that??"

Rusty sat in awkward silence, trying to find the perfect excuse for Mouth. Another voice found it instead.

"That's our movie prop."

Rusty turned, shocked to see Abigail setting down a backpack. Carson looked her over. He pulled his phone out and compared the images. "This your sister or something?"

"It's me with make-up on."

Carson nodded, not impressed, then looked down at Mouth. "Movie prop?"

"Yeah, dude. For the horror movie we're making out here. The Dillsboro Death Dealer. That's why you're here, right?"

Carson scratched his head. "Oh. You meant a *movie* movie."

"Yeah, man. What kind of movie did you think was going to happen?"

Carson awkwardly danced around the comment as Rusty cleared his throat. "I think he thought it was going to be . . . *something else.*"

Abigail looked at Carson. "Whoa, man. What kind of girl do you think I am?"

"Hopefully one like your friend?"

Abigail glared out at the idiotic young man. "Well, I'm not. But we'll let that go for now. Do you still want to be in the movie or what?"

Carson looked them over, then eyed Mouth.

"I guess. People say I sort of look like Brad Pitt."

"If by sort of, they mean not even fucking close. Other than that, you look just like him, Achilles."

Carson seemed unaffected by the diss. Instead, he did his best Hollywood stance and grinned at Abigail. "So, what do you need me to do?"

"You're a guy walking in the woods and then . . . " She moved her hand toward Mouth. "A Mouth Monster eats you."

"Sick! So, like, what's my motivation?"

"To get fucking eaten, dude!"

Carson nodded. "Let's do it!"

Abigail grinned. *Okay. Let's do it.*

"I need you to stand at the edge of the prop. We'll be right here with the camera and . . . we'll make it look like you fall in."

Carson nodded again. "Fucking movie magic!"

"Fuckin' movie magic." Abigail took a few steps back and placed the camera as Carson stood in place. She directed him with her hands, backing him up. Motioning him sideways. She looked through the lens and grinned. "Perfect. Rolling and . . . **ACTION**."

They watched as Carson awkwardly stood still. "Now what?"

"Now pretend you're falling in, dude."

"Right." Carson began swaying and going completely

overboard with his acting. Abigail used this moment to pick up the camera and slowly push in on Carson Wiseau. Then, she called out her next bit of direction, which confused the hell out of the oblivious creeper.

"Do you even remember what you did to Vanessa?"

Carson stopped moving and peered out at Abigail.

"We had a good time."

"*You* had a good time. Like you did with all the other ones."

He shook his head and threw his hands up. "I don't know what this is but—"

Abigail called out to the hole.

"Hey, Mouth. You hungry?"

The ground shook at the sound of Abigail's voice, much to the shock and awe of Carson. "Wait, wha—"

"Eat."

Rusty tried to interject. "Mouth . . . no—"

But before Carson could even pull back, Mouth shook the ground with massive force, knocking the young man off the edge and into his teeth. Local sex pest Carson screamed the entire time he was being eaten.

Abigail lowered the camera and looked over at the extremely shocked face of Rusty.

"You . . . you killed him!" Rusty said, trying his best to hold back his insides.

"No. Mouth killed him."

"You both killed him!"

She thought about it and looked over at Rusty's pale face. *Shit.* "Sorry, man. Are you mad?"

"*Yes.* Extremely."

She shrugged and pointed down. "But . . . now you don't have to worry about *that* for seven more days."

Rusty stared back in confusion, unaware of what Abigail was implying. Then he followed her pointing finger and his eyes grew wide. *That* would be the gigantic cracks spewing from all sides of Mouth. Clumps of fresh dirt were strewn about; they smelled rancid. Like the soil itself was thrown *off* something instead of *from* something.

As if . . . Mouth was angry . . . and trying to dig himself out.

Rusty was too wrapped up in Carson's shenanigans to even

notice everything. How long had it been like that? Days? Weeks? For the first time since his new life began, Rusty feared Mouth. His new friend was clearly more than just teeth in the ground.

And that fact was terrifying.

He tried to form words through his dropped jaw, but he could only muster a stutter or two. Abigail put her hand on his shoulder and nodded.

"Everything is going to be okay, Rusty. I have a plan."

"A . . . a plan? Did it involve you killing someone on camera?!"

"Sort of. It was all mostly just a bit to get *him* out here."

Rusty stared back, shocked by Abigail's reveal.

"A . . . bit?"

He shook his head, eyed the camera, then collapsed on the tarp he had brought for Mouth. Abigail let out a deep sigh and smiled down at Mouth.

"It worked, didn't it?"

MOUTH
THE
MOVIE
PROP

MOUTH WAS STILL thinking about his friend Rusty helping him out.

His old friend Wayne would have never taken the time to get something out of his teeth. He only spent his time putting things *in* them. And truthfully, Mouth didn't mind. He liked to eat, *whatever* it was. But that last time was different.

He'd been in real pain and Rusty could tell. Heck, even the other voice could tell. The voice that never stopped talking and who was suddenly obsessed with pointing that *thing* at him. Mouth tried to understand what she meant when she said, "Smile for the camera".

He didn't even know what a smile was. So, he just assumed she meant for him to shake the ground. That's what he would usually do when she would talk to him. But he didn't know if that was ever the right thing to do.

He only knew hunger, friendship, and pain. And the hunger was taking over. He hadn't had his special treat in many sleeps, and he was starting to change because of it. He could feel the ground cracking around his hunger rumbles. He was changing.

Growing.

And now there was something else. Approaching feet and a new voice. Not like the other voices he knew and trusted. This one was different. This one made Mouth uneasy.

This voice did not belong here.

This voice was not his friend.

He wanted to eat the new voice. He wanted to—

"Hey, Mouth. You hungry?"

Mouth was so excited by Abigail's question that he immediately started shaking, completely ignoring his friend Rusty's command.

He was hungry. And the voice named Carson was on the menu tonight.

"Eat."

Mouth thought back to how his friends had taken care of him. He wanted to return the favor. He wanted to take care of them . . . by taking care of Carson. So he listened to his friend Abigail and shook the man right into him. Mouth clamped down and chewed on the voice slower than he usually did.

He did not like Carson.

But he liked the way he tasted.

Mouth finished the meal and noticed Abigail staring down at him. He thought long and hard and stretched both sides of his teeth, hoping he finally gave Abigail the smile thing she had been asking for.

She smiled back and said—

"It worked, didn't it?"

THERE
BE
MONSTERS

Rusty paced back and forth.

He hadn't said a word in a good ten minutes. Just a steady flow of pacing right next to Mouth. Abigail tried to explain what happened and why. After a few sentences, she popped a squat on the ground and waited for whatever would happen next. Finally, he stopped and stared at her.

"We just killed somebody!"

"Did not. He fell in the hole, man."

Rusty pointed his fingers in a fatherly manner. "You used Mouth to help yourself."

"Umm. To help *both* of us. And so many other people!" She shook her head and threw her hands up. "That guy has hurt so many girls . . . and this town just lets him get away with it."

"But we can't just—"

"Fuck that. He came all the way out here because I sent one sexy picture. He was a bad guy. And now, he's a no guy."

Rusty stared down at Mouth, flabbergasted by Abigail. "How can you be so nonchalant about this?

"Again. He was a bad guy. He hurt my friend Vanessa." She threw her hands up. "This town is welcome. You're welcome!"

"That was reckless! And for what?" Rusty once again picked up his pacing routine. "What's your grand plan here with the camera and Mouth and whatever this was, Abigail?"

The confident teen finally seemed nervous and uncomfortable for the first time. "I sort of want to make a documentary."

"A what?"

"A documentary. You know, like a true story."

"I know what a documentary is."

She sat in silence as he continued to pace around. "I mean, you asked." The anger seemed to leave his face, replaced with curiosity.

"Documentaries are about important things," he said.

She laughed. "Not all of them. Seriously. Have you ever seen *Winnebago Man*? That shit is funny." She rubbed her head and grinned. "*I appreciate that very much, Tony. DON'T SLAM THE FUCKING DOOR.*"

Rusty stopped pacing and stared at her.

"Sorry, it's from *Winneb*—look, man. This *is* important. You said it yourself; you wished people could see this. We could show them."

"Then they'll come for us and for him," Rusty said, shaking his head.

"Impossible, dude. They won't."

"How?"

"People will never know who or where we are. But they'll know about Wayne and the others. And they'll know about Mouth. But the way we want them to know about him."

He looked over at the bloody teeth in the ground and held his hands out. "Why's this so important to you?"

She walked over to Mouth and stared into him.

"Because sometimes life is pretty terrible. And bad things happen to good things. We don't all have to be who they want us to be or who they taught us to be. We can all change, but we have to have a fresh start. We can only do that by having *a chance* for a fresh start."

"What are you saying, exactly?"

"You're hiding from something. I'm hiding from something. We bring whatever that is here to Mouth. And we purge them."

Rusty shook his head. "Just to be clear, this purging ceremony you're talking about is us feeding two more people to Mouth."

"Well, that implies that we both only have one person each that we want to—"

"Abigail."

A long deep sigh. "Yes. *That* is what I'm implying. All three of us need a fresh start. And we've been brought together by this crazy, moviemaking asshole who created an actual monster."

"Created him?"

"Like Victor Frankenstein himself." Abigail walked over to her backpack and dumped a pile of Wayne's videotapes on the ground. "I watched them all. Mouth used to be small. Like, real small."

She picked up one tape and held it out. "This was the first time he fed Mouth. That Rand guy." She formed her hand into a small cup shape. "And your buddy Wayne force-fed him to Mouth. Both feet, ankle first! It was fucking crazy! You should totally watch it. Anyway, that's exactly when he started growing. And now—"

She threw her hands up, presenting the new size of the teeth beast. Cracks splintering out from the earth. "We all need a fresh start. We can prove Mouth doesn't have to eat people anymore."

"You literally just fed him a person, Abigail."

"Yeah, I know. But that was for a good reason. And the next one will be as well. We can't cold turkey the teeth, Rusty. And we can't keep running from whatever the hell we're both running from."

He stared back at her and scratched his head. "What if he had a family? That was a person. And now he isn't because of us. I don't know how I feel about that. *And you.* You're just so calm about it."

Abigail sighed, then walked over to Rusty, nodding the entire time.

"I'm not calm, Rusty. I'm inspired. That dude Carson was King fucking Sex Creep. *A monster.* Just like Wayne. And just like whatever the hell it is for you." She grinned. "So, we're going to feed our monsters to the teeth in the ground. And after that? We all start fresh."

She stared back at Rusty, seemingly unsure of where his head was.

"So. Tell me about your monster, Rust."

JEKYLL

AND

HIDE

RUSTY HADN'T THOUGHT about that night in a long time.

It was the night *everything* came crashing down in his life. And what led him to roaming around. And ultimately, the night that landed him here, telling Abigail about the night his wife left him.

"I'm my own monster, Abigail. That's the truth of it all."

The odd pair sat in the living room, sharing a pizza and some soda. Abigail was devouring her second slice before he had even touched his first. This story had been weighing on him for years. And that kind of weight couldn't be swayed by a greasy slice of pie.

"Bullshit, man. There has to be someone out there that wronged you."

He nodded.

"Laurie used to tell me I was just like Jekyll and Hyde."

Abigail sat up, slice in one hand, the other a clenched fist. "*I've played with dangerous knowledge!*"

Rusty ignored her impression and continued to hang his head low. Abigail sunk back into her cushion and picked at the edge of a crispy pepperoni. "Sorry, man."

"I had a pretty serious drinking problem. One she tried to point out repeatedly. But, you know, that's the thing about problems. They stick around unless you're willing to do something about 'em."

"Bad time for me to refer back to us feeding Mouth creepo Carson?" He stared straight ahead. *Yes.*

She sunk even lower. "Right."

"I refused to change or to even try to change. Just stubborn as hell. Hated when people tried to stop me from doing something I liked doing. And I liked drinking."

"Did you love her?"

Rusty looked up at Abigail, glossy eyes staring back.

"At one point, but things change. That's the best part about the bottle. It never changes, it just gets refilled. Anyway, she'd never know which version of me would be waiting at home. And then one night, I had to pick her up from work. I don't exactly remember why but I had been drinking and—"

"Hyde picked her up?"

Rusty gave a small nod, then wiped his eyes. "That's where my small limp comes from. Wrapped us around a telephone pole. She finally walked out on me when her legs started working again. But she should've done it *long* before that night."

"I'm sorry, Rusty."

He wiped his eyes again.

"Don't be. She's out there living the *happily ever after* she always wanted. And I haven't touched a bottle since." He finally took a bite out of a waiting pizza slice. "So, see, the only monster I had to get rid of was my Hyde. And I'd like to think I've already done that."

"Well shit, man."

He sat back in his chair and scratched his beard with his free hand. "Sorry to ruin your purge plans."

She perked up. "Ruin? Are you kidding me? I'm still taking my turn."

"Can we maybe not refer to it like that?"

"How do you want me to describe this particular thing, Rust?"

He let out an awkward sigh and took a bite of pizza. She was watching his every move.

"What?"

"What if you're a different character in that story now?" She asked.

"What story?"

She wiped her hands free of pizza and sat up. "*Dr. Jekyll and Mr. Hyde.*"

"What do you mean?"

"Think back on the movie."

Rusty's face shrunk. "That was a long time ago."

"I know. 1931. Same year as *Dracula* and *Frankenstein*. But you remember those, right?"

"Well, obviously."

She shook her head and took offense. "Obviously? Well, *obviously* you need to put some respect on Rouben Mamoulian, dude. *Queen Christina* with Greta Garbo. Fucking Greta Garbo, my guy! *Becky Sharp*! *The Mark of Zorro*! *Blood and—*"

"Abigail."

"Right, sorry." She took a deep breath and folded her hands in front of her face. "The point is, what if you're Dr. Lanyon now, man. The guy that discovers and causes the death of the actual Jekyll and Hyde."

"And who is that supposed to be?"

Abigail leaned back into the couch and let out a deep sigh.

"My piece of shit stepfather."

ABIGAIL'S
SKELETON

ABIGAIL PACED BACK AND FORTH.

The pizza box was damn near empty at this point. And the coffee table looked like a group of teen boys had left empty soda cans all over the place. She talked to herself like a drug addict working something out in her head.

"So, there's bad people, right? And then there are *evil* people. Sure, Manson and the like could fit in that label but I'm talking every day normal people. The kind that wear masks in public, then take them off in private. I'm talking about people who are just mean for the sake of being mean. Kick dogs, punch wives. Beat their stepdaughter black and blue all while trashing all her dead dad's leftover belongings. That's Bob Mahoney. And he's the worst person in the world."

"Where is he now?"

She shrugged and plopped back down on the couch.

"I'm assuming still in the old house up near Anderson. But I don't know for sure."

"And when's the last time you saw him?"

"When I shot him in the leg."

Rusty stared back in shock—

"When you what?!"

"I was just protecting my mom. I was always trying to protect her. He had just gone on one of his classic *beat-the-hell-out-of-Abigail* routines. It carried over to her. And it was even more vicious because I guess he figured she was an adult. She could handle it, right? He didn't know about the little gun my dad had. So, I limped down there and shot him. I was aiming for his head, but I grew up watching stormtroopers, you know what I mean?"

Rusty let out a sigh and shook his head. "How old were you?"

"Fifteen . . . but I was turning sixteen that next week. So, I didn't get *that* birthday cake. I packed what I could that night and ran away. Hollywood, baby! That's how I ended up here in Dillsboro."

"Did he call the police?"

"Bob wasn't a police guy. And they'd probably want to know

why his wife had a bowling ball growing out of the side of her head. Plus, he didn't want me to go to jail. At least, that's what I gathered from him screaming 'I'll kill you when I find you' as I walked out the front door with all my shit."

"And that's why he's your fresh start. Because he's looking for you. Still."

"People like that don't give up, Rust. And it's not just about me. My mom needs a fresh start as well."

"When's the last time you talked to her?"

Abigail sunk deeper into the couch. "It's been a few weeks. I'd call once a week to check in . . . but she started to get nervous. Like he knew that she knew where I was. I'm worried for her, Rusty." She wiped her eyes. "You took care of your monster. Help me with mine."

Rusty stared back at Abigail. He had been carrying around so much hurt and pain for years, that it was hard to see what that looked like on other people. He could now see it as clear as day on her face. She *did* need his help just as much as he needed this friendship.

He had suddenly found himself caring about another human for the first time in nearly a decade. He found himself wanting to make up for all the wrong he had done in his previous life. All the chaos. All the pain. The burning wreckage of an old relationship. He wanted to make up for all of it.

And if that meant helping Abigail kill her monster, then so be it. The world would be a much better place with one less asshole in it. And maybe that was the point of all this anyway. The point of Wayne. The point of Mouth. And the point of a fresh start. The world revolved around hope and who you could give it to. Rusty understood that now.

And he wanted to give Abigail all the hope in the world.

CYCLE GHOULS PROP MASKS

BOB **MAHONEY KNEW** he was an absolute motherfucker.

He never wanted to be an elementary school principal. But that was just the way his life shook out. A lot of drinking and anger, mixed with hundreds of children screaming, laughing, and running. That sort of thing would drive anyone crazy.

So, he was happy that he didn't have to live that life anymore. Especially after the leg injury. He couldn't imagine trying to make it down those glossy hallways on crutches, all while dodging little Ben or Suzy Snotnose.

He was happy to be done with that life.

Now he just collected disability checks and searched online for his runaway stepdaughter. Little Abigail Mahoney. By his count, she'd been gone for just about three years. Hightailed it right out of town after she shot him in the leg protecting her bitch mom. He almost gave up looking a couple years back just out of the fact that he assumed she was dead. Or street trash.

She deserved that sort of life.

Abigail was weak and a constant victim. And she was alone. Hell, she had never even been to the mall by herself. Never even out of town! She ran away with no money, friends, or family. She had nothing and she ran out into the jaws of society ill prepared.

The world ate people like that alive.

It chewed them up and spat them out. He laughed at the thought of her thinking she could survive without any help. Sure, he beat her from time to time, but he kept a roof over her head. Fed and clothed her. He wasn't *that* bad of a guy. But now he figured, he *was* that bad of a guy. Or he *would* be if he ever found her.

Bob had a solid lead on her whereabouts a few months back, but lost track not too long after. That was as close as he had ever been. Figured it would be as close as he would ever get. The thought alone made him thirsty and angry.

He pulled himself out of the old, flowered recliner and grabbed his cane. He limped over to the kitchen, set his cane on the counter, and poured another glass of bourbon. Nothing good. Just whatever got the job done. That was all he believed in.

Getting the job done.

He took a swig and turned to face the rest of the house. That was when he saw the two masked invaders staring back at him. But they weren't wearing normal home invasion type of masks. These were different. Two cheap-as-hell looking ghost masks. Like something a kid in the seventies would wear trick-or-treating.

"Who the hell are you supposed to be?"

"Ghosts of Christmas Past."

Bob perked up at the voice and let out a small, taunting laugh. "Abigail?"

Abigail lifted the mask, revealing her angry face. She ignored Rusty's audible confusion at revealing her identity. She was only focused on her monster.

"Hey, Bob. What's new?"

"You have to be the stupidest little asshole in the world coming back here."

Abigail watched his every move as Bob sized up Rusty.

"Where's my mom?" She asked, desperate for an answer.

Bob shrugged and took another pull of his bourbon. "Sleeping somewhere around here."

She called out—

"MOM!"

Rusty shook his head. "What was the point of the masks, Abigail?"

"They look menacing."

Bob laughed. "They don't. They look shitty."

"You look shitty, Bob. These are original screen used!" She focused on the other rooms behind her. "MOM!"

There was still no answer, so she decided to roam through the house, leaving Bob and Rusty alone.

"MOM!"

She made her way through the full downstairs, then headed upstairs.

"MOM! I'm home!"

Abigail grew nervous as she called out for her mom again. She stopped in front of the slightly ajar bedroom door. She could see the shape of a woman laying in the bed. Abigail smiled in relief as she pushed her way into the room.

"Mom! I'm home! We came to . . . "

She stopped when she noticed the dried blood on the off-white comforter.

"Mom?"

Once she reached the bed, she put her hand on the sleeping woman's shoulder and nudged her. "Mommy?"

Abigail put more force on the second tug, causing the stiff body to fall flat. Then . . . she screamed the loudest scream she had ever mustered.

The right side of her mother's head was caved in. The rest of her face was unrecognizable.

Abigail caressed the dead face of her mother as she cried her eyes out. "I'm so sorry for leaving you here. I'm sorry for leaving you with . . . him."

Abigail shifted her focus on what was outside of the bedroom door and waiting down in the kitchen. She looked around the room and her eyes fell on the nightstand closest to where her mother had been laying. A stone Rooster statue stared back. Her eyes watered at it, knowing it belonged on the mantle above the fireplace.

She walked over and picked it up to see dried blood and strands of hair. She gave her mom one last look and walked out of the bedroom, gripping the statue as tight as she could.

Back downstairs, Abigail walked into the kitchen and stared back at the odd pair. Rusty was the first to speak up—

"Abigail? Everything . . . "

His voice trailed off when he saw the rage in her face. And the weapon in her hand. He looked over at Bob staring back with his bloated, drunk face. Then—

"You motherfucker!!! YOU MOTHERFUCKER!"

Abigail rushed over to Bob and smashed the Rooster statue into the side of his head, knocking the old man to the ground. Once he was down, she kicked and punched him repeatedly, her pain powering her every move.

Rusty finally pulled her away from the unconscious Bob and held her as she cried. "We should go."

Abigail pulled away and looked up at him, teary-eyed, broken, and speechless.

"We can take 'em both, if you want. We don't have to leave her here."

Abigail wiped her face, grateful for the suggestion.

"Go wait in the car. I'll get them out there," Rusty assured her.

Abigail nodded, then slid her *Cycle Ghoul* mask down over her face, smearing one side of it with her mother's blood. Then, she walked out of the house. It was almost time for that fresh start.

But first, it was time to feed the teeth in the ground.

"There was no coming back from that."

BOB THE BLOB

RUSTY TRIED HIS best not to look over at Abigail.

She didn't say one word on the entire drive back from the Mahoney house. She just stared straight ahead, lost in her pain. He recognized that look. That feeling. And she stayed like that as they walked through the woods, heading out to Mouth.

He also knew that what they were about to do wasn't going to change any of it. But it would help in the short term, and that was fine with him. He cocked a look behind him to see Bob tied up and still unconscious on a sled he found in the garage. That would make having a conversation about everything so much easier. No whimpering or pleading from Bob. Just two friends having a nice talk.

Finally, Rusty looked over at her. "You said your dad introduced you to movies, right?"

She stayed silent but gave a slight nod.

"But did your mom keep that love going?"

Her eyes watered with another nod. *Yes.*

"What was the first movie y'all ever saw together? Like sat down and just experienced at home?"

"*Jaws.*"

Rusty gave his own nod. "That's a good one."

"Good one? It's the greatest movie ever fucking made, dude."

Rusty let out a small laugh—

"You say that about a lot of them."

"Yeah, so? Movies are the best. They're the greatest gift we've ever been given. Can you imagine where humanity would be without them? Can you?"

"Listening to a lot more music?"

"We would be fucking lost, man. LOST. Movies make people feel alive. They make people fall in love. They make people scared and not feel alone. They make people dream. They make people question who they are and what they could be. They're pure magic. And without them, we'd all be fucking miserable. I mean JESUS, dude. Your fucking pal Wayne fed a dude to Mouth because he took movies away from *him*. That's what life without movies is like." She wiped a tear from her eye. "That's what life without her will be like."

The pair continued to pull Bob closer to Mouth. Rusty looked over at Abigail.

"It was *The Blob* for me. The original. And it scared the hell out of me. And my mom laughed for weeks that I was so scared of this ridiculous thing. Hid my face behind a pillow and all."

Abigail stopped in her tracks. "First of all, *The Blob* is not ridiculous. Chuck Russell's *The Blob* was nightmare fuel, but still. Regardless of what version, what makes the blob scary is that it just destroys anything and everything. It doesn't give a shit. Just like Bob here. *Bob the Blob.*"

Rusty pulled the sled into the clearing. He looked over at Abigail and rubbed his beard.

"You know we don't have to do this, right? We can just turn him into the police."

She sighed and looked back at him.

"Then he'll just get out. That's not an option, Rust. You saw what he did to her. What he'll do to me if he can."

Rusty gave a nod. He did see and that image would stay in his head forever. So, he couldn't really judge Abigail for feeling the way she did. Plus, he had no interest in putting her life in danger.

"Okay then."

A mutual nod.

"Okay then."

Rusty walked over and kicked Bob in the ribs, startling him awake. The beaten man looked around at his surroundings. He yelled out from behind his taped mouth, so Rusty bent down to pull it off. Abigail stopped him.

"Keep it on. He doesn't get any last words."

Bob shot a look of fear at Abigail, probably realizing that the world had not in fact eaten her up like he had hoped. It had only made her stronger. *Scarier.*

But had it made her a killer? He muffled his final words out slowly.

"You can't kill me, Abigail. Your bark doesn't have any bite."

She grinned—

"Nope, but his does."

Abagail nodded down at Mouth as Bob tried to muffle more

words out. She placed his body at the edge so his head would be the first thing to go in.

"It's time to eat, Mouth."

The ground shook with excitement as Abigail and Rusty took a step back. Bob kicked and screamed as best he could as Mouth shook him off the edge. Abigail didn't take her eyes off the feast until every bit of her monster Bob Mahoney was eaten by the teeth in the ground.

There was no coming back from that.

Abigail sat alone with Mouth. Rusty had gone back to the car to collect her mom's dead body, so she figured she had some time to talk to her only other friend.

"This next one is special. I need you to treat her . . . different. I don't even know if you'll understand what I'm about to say, but I want to say it anyway. I think you need to hear it, Mouth."

The ground vibrated slightly around her. She gave a small smile.

"Some people are born monsters. Others are turned into them. Your old friend Wayne turned you into one. Your last meal turned me into one. And well, something else did it to Rusty. But he changed and I want you to know you can change as well. *I can change.* We don't have to be these things that they turned us into, okay?"

Another small rumble. She dug into her back pocket and pulled out a folded piece of paper. Her eyes watered as she looked it over.

"My mom knew I was going to leave. She didn't know it was going to go the way it did, but she knew it was going to happen. It wasn't until a few months later that I found this note she slipped in my bag. So, I'm going to read it to you because it helped me. And I think it can help you. I want to help you."

She cleared her throat and wiped a tear away from her eye—

"*I know change is scary but it's also exciting and . . . it shows us what being alive truly means. It's okay to have every emotion, but you always have to have faith that everything will work out. You have to find something to live for when everything else is falling apart. You have to find a reason to be the bright light in the darkness . . . because it will eat you alive. It can snuff out your joy. Don't let it. Be the best version of yourself and everything else will fall into place. And you'll finally be able to be who you're meant to be.*" She choked up. "*A gift to the world.*"

She brought the letter down and stared directly into the hole.

"You're a gift to the world, Mouth. No more eating people. No more being this thing you were turned into. Or turning into. It's time for a fresh start. It's time to be the best version of ourselves."

She gave an *and that's that*-type nod, and the ground gave a slight rumble back. She turned to see Rusty holding the body of her mom. She choked up again and delivered a kiss to the top of her sheet-covered head.

Abigail whispered her goodbyes and looked at Rusty.

"Thank you, Rust."

He nodded, then she turned her back on Mouth, Rusty, and her mom.

"You can do it now," she said, fighting through tears. So, Rusty took a few steps and gently placed the body on the edge of the hole. He then slid her inside Mouth . . . and watched.

He was mystified by the fact that Mouth seemed to be placing a great deal of care on the body. Like the teeth were guiding her gently down, instead of turning her into a whirlwind of blood and gore. The teeth had compassion. And Rusty realized that maybe Abigail was right. A fresh start was truly possible for all three of them. And that thought alone made him break down in tears as he finally lost touch of the body. Mouth had her from here.

Mouth had *all* of them from here.

FRESH START

RUSTY **NERVOUSLY ORGANIZED** the old barn that Wayne mostly used as a garage-slash-storage space.

At least, that was what he always thought it was. He was shocked to discover the old barn could easily be converted into a living area. It already had a small kitchen and a loft that could be a bedroom. He figured with a little money and a lot of effort; he could turn this into *something*.

So, he got to work.

He updated the water pipes and faucets. He changed out a broken window in the loft. He cleared out all the trash and cobwebs, swept every inch of the floor, and changed some of the old lightbulbs out. He moved in some of the furniture he wasn't using from the house. A coffee table. A nice couch. A recliner. A small dinner table with chairs.

He took all the shelves out of the secret basement room and set them up along the old barn walls. He took all the old movie props and memorabilia out and gave them homes in there as well. Same with the collection of videotapes.

He took a step back and looked the place over. The makeover was mostly complete, and it only took him about three weeks. He gave the space a nod and smiled. He opened the side door and walked out into the sunshine.

"What are you doing in there, ya creep?"

Rusty spun around, shocked to see Abigail staring back at him. "Nothing."

She squinted her eyes and nodded. "Sure."

"What are you doing?"

She took out a book from behind her and held it up. It was an old copy of Mary Shelley's *Frankenstein*. "I was just reading this to Mouth. He seems to like it."

Rusty grinned and gave his nod of approval. *Don't we all.*

"Also, the ground seems to be getting better. He's doing just fine."

"What's it been? Three or so weeks without . . . ?"

She tilted her head. "That sounds about right."

"You got him to change."

"Or I'm just feeding him all my enemies when you go to sleep."

Rusty thought about this for a moment, then gave her a serious look.

"Abigail?"

"I'm just fucking with you, dude. He's good. I think we're all good."

A mutual nod of agreement.

"So, what now?" Rusty asked, curious about her new life plans.

Abigail wavered and looked over at her car. "I guess I should probably get out of here and find a new job. A new place to live. A new hobby that doesn't involve feeding a subterranean mouth thing."

"About that. Let me show you something." He nodded toward the barn door. So, she slowly walked over, curious as can be. Rusty held the door open for her as she walked in and looked around.

Her face lit up at the barn makeover. And the organization. And, well, *everything*.

"Whoa! Look at this place."

"You kept saying stuff about fresh starts, right? How 'bout a free place to live."

She looked over at him in shock.

"Are you serious?"

"I figured you help feed Mouth. That can be your job."

She laughed and shook her head.

"I need a job that pays, Rust."

"I'd pay you. And you don't need a job. That'll take away all your time."

"Yes, I'm so busy." The sarcasm radiated off her in the sun.

"You have a documentary to make, right?"

She looked over at the shelves filled with videotapes.

"Are you actually giving me permission to—"

"To have a fresh start. It's like your mom said, Abigail. Be the best version of yourself. I think you can do that here, doing what you've always wanted to do. Making movies." He put his hand out. "So, what do you say?"

She grinned from ear to ear and gave him a massive hug. She pulled away and stared in awe at her new creative living space.

"Thank you, Rust. I'm going to make the best movie ever fucking made."

"I thought that was *Jaws*?"

"It was. The shark is on the clock, dude."

He let out a small laugh, then gave a nod goodbye. Rusty walked out of the door, letting her be alone.

Abigail walked through the entire space and thought about everything she was about to do. About whom she was about to be. But she mostly thought about how she had plenty of room to hang ALL of her movie posters now.

And that was cool as hell.

A GIFT TO THE WORLD

MOUTH THOUGHT ABOUT his fresh start.
His pearly existence now included friends and stories.
It included new food, the kind that didn't scream.
It had more smiles and less fear.
The ground no longer rumbled.
He no longer begged for an escape.
He was at peace.
He was loved.
He was a gift to the world.
The teeth in the ground were happy.
And that's all Mouth ever wanted to be.

ACKNOWLEDGEMENTS

I wrote this book at a very chaotic and strange time in my life. There were a ton of things eating away at me that manifested themselves into a monstrous mouth in the ground. These are the people that made sure they didn't swallow me whole:

First and foremost, to my mom . . . for everything. For never pressuring me to be anything but *me*. For introducing me to movies. For *Jaws* and *Halloween*. And for encouraging your children to *always* use their imagination.

To Phoenix . . . for being my rock. For never judging me for my mistakes. Or my pursuit of happiness. For always being my first reader . . . and always listening to my ridiculous pitches. For being a wonderful human. YOU are a gift to the world.

To Sophia . . . Thank YOU for the daily joy and happiness. Thank you for being **you**.

To Tom . . . for sharing a lifetime of books with me. For always reading whatever lands in your email. For the constant feedback and support. For always supporting authors and publishers. And for always being an inspiration.

To my family and friends . . . Thank you for always encouraging and supporting this weird and wildly unpredictable path.

To the people who read this weird little thing before anyone else: Eilise, Jason, Wolfe, Nora, Meg, and Heather. You all helped shape this book into what it is today. Thank you, thank you, thank you.

To the handful of authors who have been inspiring, kind and generous with their time: Grady, Daniel, Clay, Cynthia, Eric, Hailey, Laurel, Jenny, John, Andy, J.H., Alex, Carson, Haley, Kyle, and Brian.

To Jonathan Janz . . . for taking the time to not only read an early draft, but to bring me to tears with your beautiful words about this book. You are a treasure and a wonderful human.

To Michael J. Seidlinger . . . for your friendship, support, and encouragement. For your kind words about this book. I couldn't have done any of this without you!

To Rebekah McKendry . . . for always encouraging my weirdness and supporting it. For always taking the time to read whatever comes your way. For a *Glorious* friendship. And . . . for your incredibly kind words about this book.

To Matt and Alex . . . what can I say? A glory hole brought us together . . . and we formed a much bigger hole as a group. Wait . . . ummm . . . that is . . .

ANYWAY—you both have been incredible to collaborate with on this book. Thank you for supporting such a weird story. Thank you for supporting and cultivating weird stories in general. Thank you both for being phenomenal individuals that care about art and humans. And making sure folks from all walks of life have a platform with you and Tenebrous. For always fighting the good fight. This world needs more people like you . . . and I'm lucky to call you my publisher. More so, I'm incredibly grateful to call you both my friends. New Weird Horror . . . **FOREVER**.

CONTENT WARNINGS

Being a work of mature Horror, a degree of violence, gore, sex and/or death is to be expected.

In addition, *Mouth* contains a scene of animal death.

Please be advised.

More information at
www.tenebrouspress.com

ABOUT THE CONTRIBUTORS

Joshua Hull is a screenwriter/filmmaker/author based out of Central Indiana. He's the co-screenwriter of *Glorious*, a 2022 Lovecraftian horror film starring Ryan Kwanten and J.K. Simmons. He is the author of *Underexposed!: The 50 Greatest Movies Never Made* and the horror children's book *Bedtime for Bobby*. In late 2022, he was awarded the Edward Johnson-Ott Hoosier Award for his contributions to Indiana film by the Indiana Film Journalists Association.

Halil Karasu was born and raised in Istanbul, Turkey, and grew up adoring comic books, cartoons, and slasher films. He studied graphic design at Mimar Sinan Fine Arts University.

Kristofor Harris is an artist out of Kansas City, currently working on his creator-owned series, *Ancient Cosmonauts,* and numerous other projects.

TENEBROUS PRESS

aims to drag the malleable Horror genre into newer, Weirder territory with stories that are incisive, provocative, intelligent and terrifying; delivered by voices diverse and unsung.

NEW WEIRD HORROR

FIND OUT MORE:

www.tenebrouspress.com
Social Media @TenebrousPress